# THE ADVENTURES OF
# HERCULES

A GRAPHIC NOVEL

BY MARTIN POWELL &
JOSÉ ALFONSO OCAMPO RUIZ

STONE ARCH BOOKS
A CAPSTONE IMPRINT

Graphic Revolve is published by Stone Arch Books
A Capstone Imprint
1710 Roe Crest Drive, North Mankato, Minnesota 56003
www.capstonepub.com

Cataloging-in-Publication Data is available at the Library
of Congress website.
Hardcover ISBN: 978-1-4965-0019-9
Paperback ISBN: 978-1-4342-1384-6

Summary: Born of a mortal woman and the king of the
gods, Hercules is blessed with extraordinary strength.
The goddess Hera commands that the mighty Hercules
must undergo twelve incredible tasks to pay for a
mistake he made in the past.

Common Core back matter written by Dr. Katie Monnin.

Color by Jorge Gonzalez.

Designer: Bob Lentz
Assistant Designer: Peggie Carley
Editor: Donald Lemke
Assistant Editor: Sean Tulien
Creative Director: Heather Kindseth
Editorial Director: Michael Dahl
Publisher: Ashley C. Andersen Zantop

Printed in the United States of America in
Stevens Point, Wisconsin.
052014          008092WZF14

# TABLE OF CONTENTS

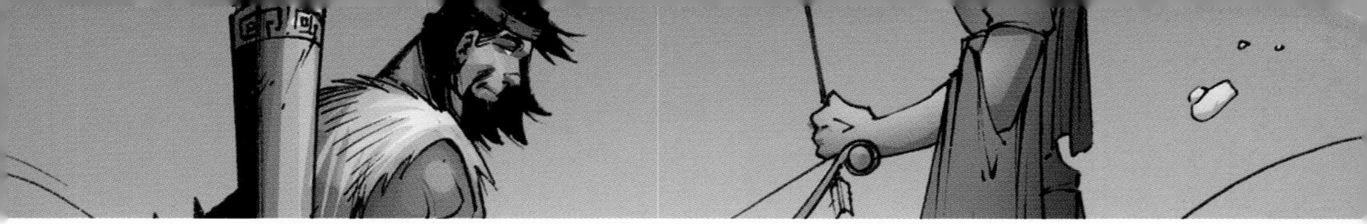

# ABOUT HERCULES

In Greek and Roman times, Hercules was one of the most celebrated mythical figures. Half human and half god, Hercules was the son of Zeus, the king of the gods, and Alcmene, a mortal woman. The goddess Hera, Zeus's wife, was angry that Zeus had fathered children with another woman. Since Hera could not harm Zeus, she punished his son Hercules instead.

When Zeus learned that Alcmene was pregnant with Hercules, he announced that the next child born would be the new king. To ruin Zeus's plan, Hera caused a boy named Eurystheus to be born early, making him king instead of Hercules. This angered Zeus, but he stuck to his word and made Eurystheus king. Hera had robbed Hercules of his throne — and her revenge had only just begun.

Next, Hera made Hercules go temporarily insane. In this state, he did some horrible things. When he came to his senses, he visited the Oracle to find out how to redeem himself. Unfortunately, the Oracle was also being manipulated by Hera. The Oracle told him to serve King Eurystheus by performing twelve difficult labors.

Years later, Hera once again sent a madness down upon Hercules. In his altered state of mind, he threw his best friend Iphitus over a wall, killing him. When Hercules realized what had happened, he pledged himself to Queen Omphale of Lydia. Again he hoped to atone for his tragic mistake, not knowing he was innocent.

After serving Omphale for a year, Hercules was free to do as he pleased. He went to the town of Thebes and married a woman named Deianira. The two of them raised a family together. One day, a centaur named Nessus kidnapped Deianira. Hercules managed to shoot Nessus with an arrow tipped with poison from the blood of the Hydra. Near death, Nessus told Deianira to rub his blood on Hercules, which would make Hercules love her forever. But Nessus had lied to her — his blood was poisoned from the arrow Hercules had shot him with, and the poisoned blood burned Hercules's flesh.

As he died, Hercules was allowed into Olympus, the home of the gods, as a reward for his good deeds — and as consolation for being the victim of Hera's trickery.

# CAST OF CHARACTERS

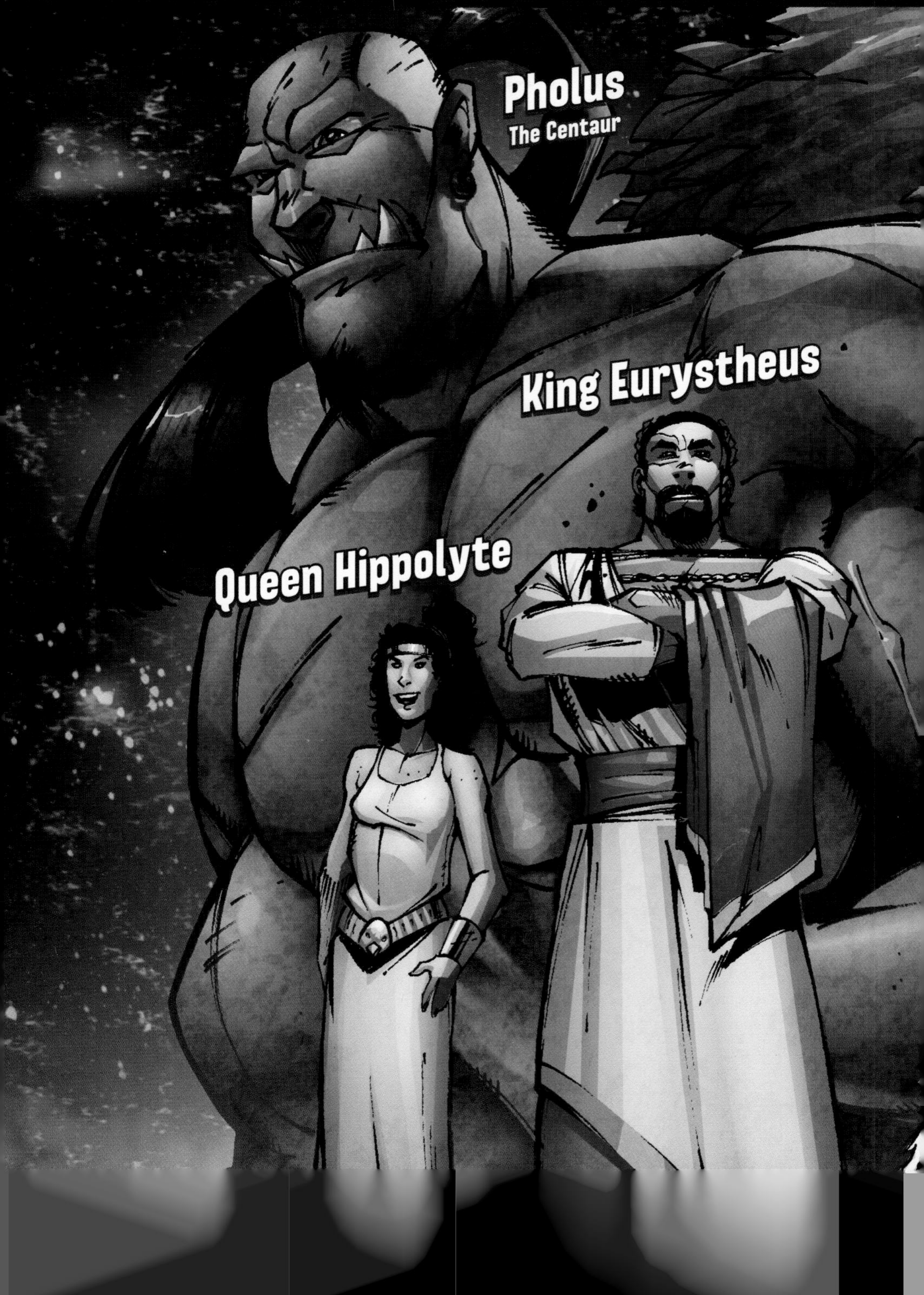
Pholus
The Centaur
King Eurystheus
Queen Hippolyte

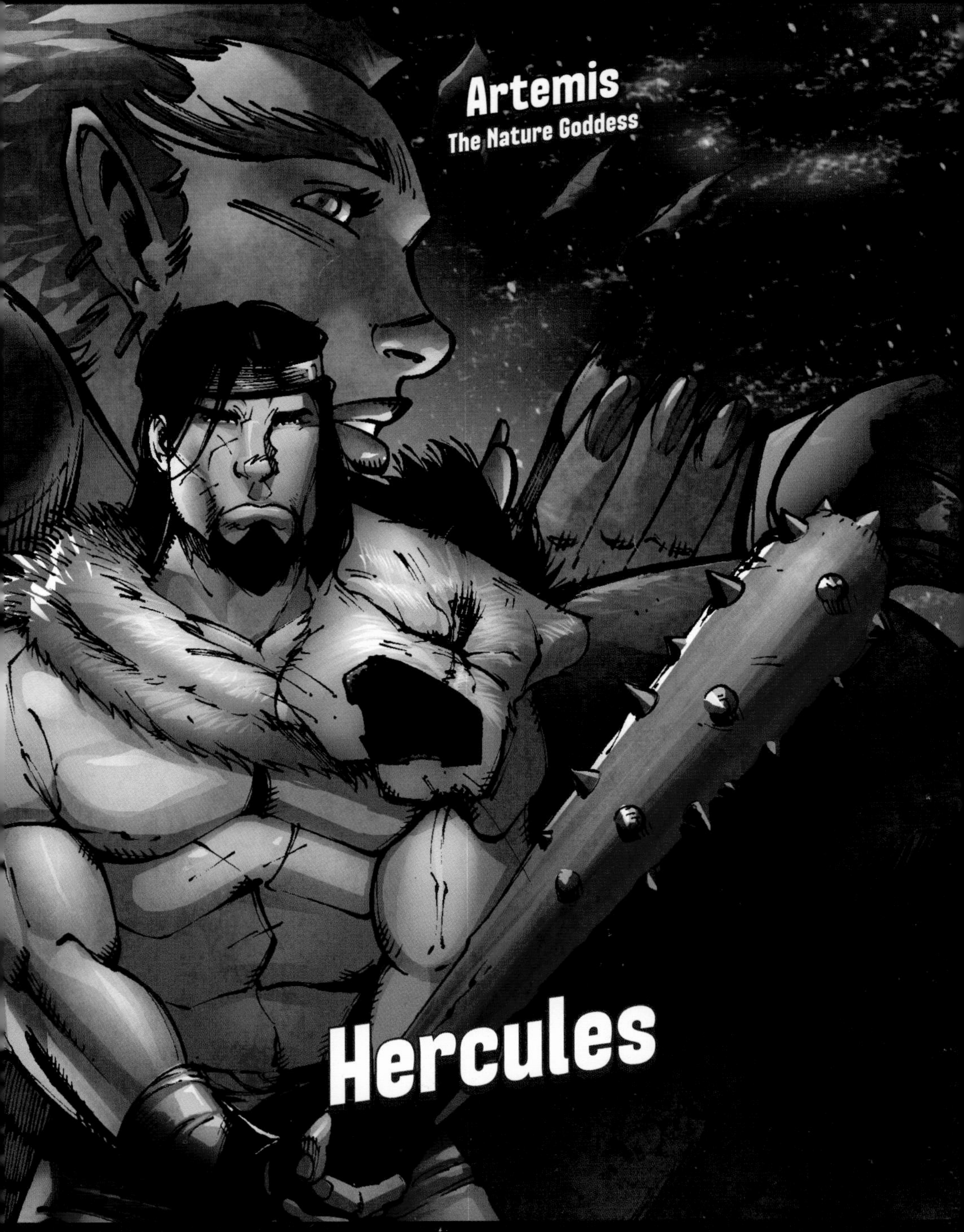
Artemis
The Nature Goddess
Hercules

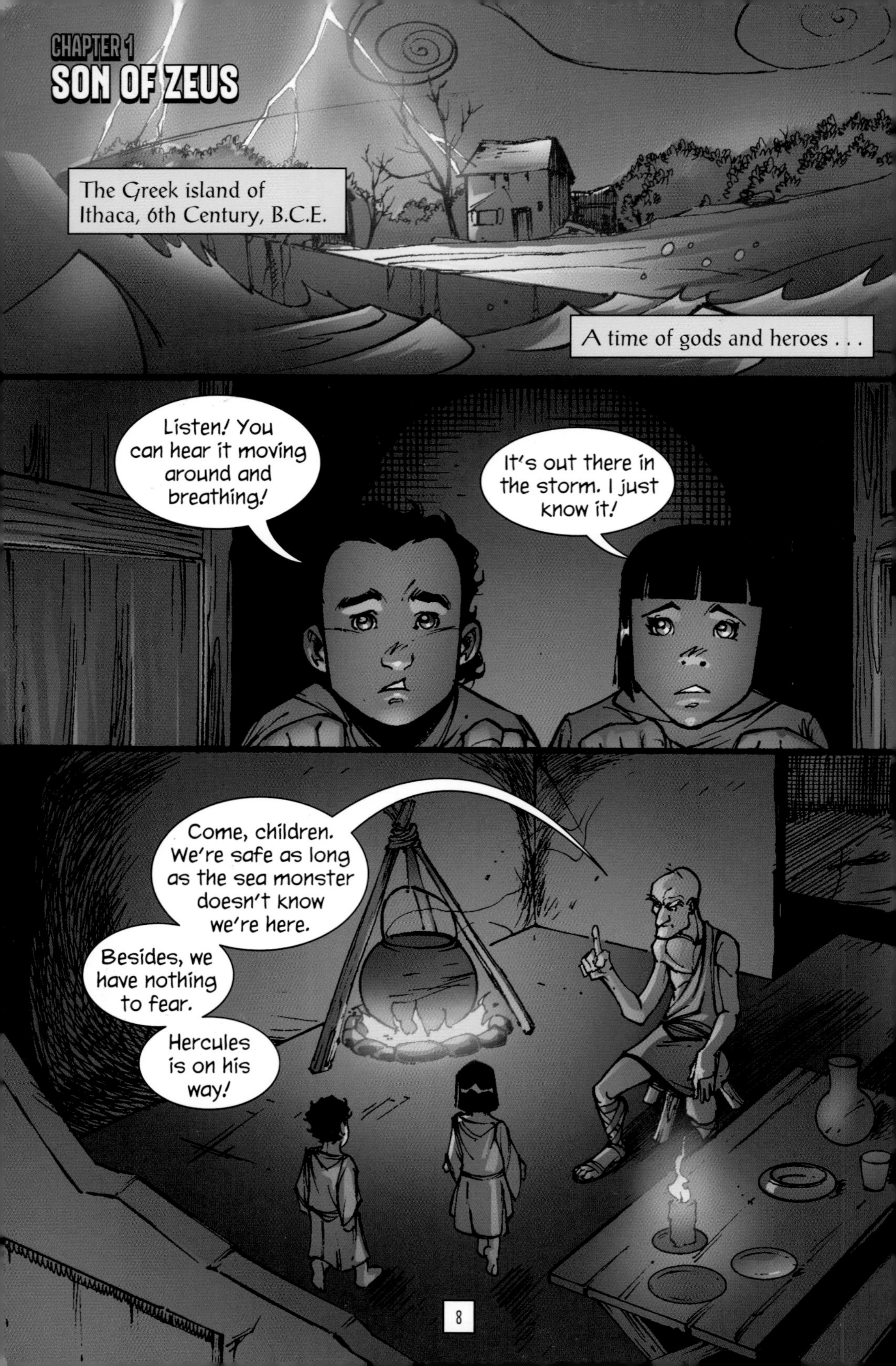
CHAPTER 1
SON OF ZEUS
The Greek island of Ithaca, 6th Century, B.C.E.
A time of gods and heroes . . .
Listen! You can hear it moving around and breathing!
It's out there in the storm. I just know it!
Come, children. We're safe as long as the sea monster doesn't know we're here.
Besides, we have nothing to fear.
Hercules is on his way!

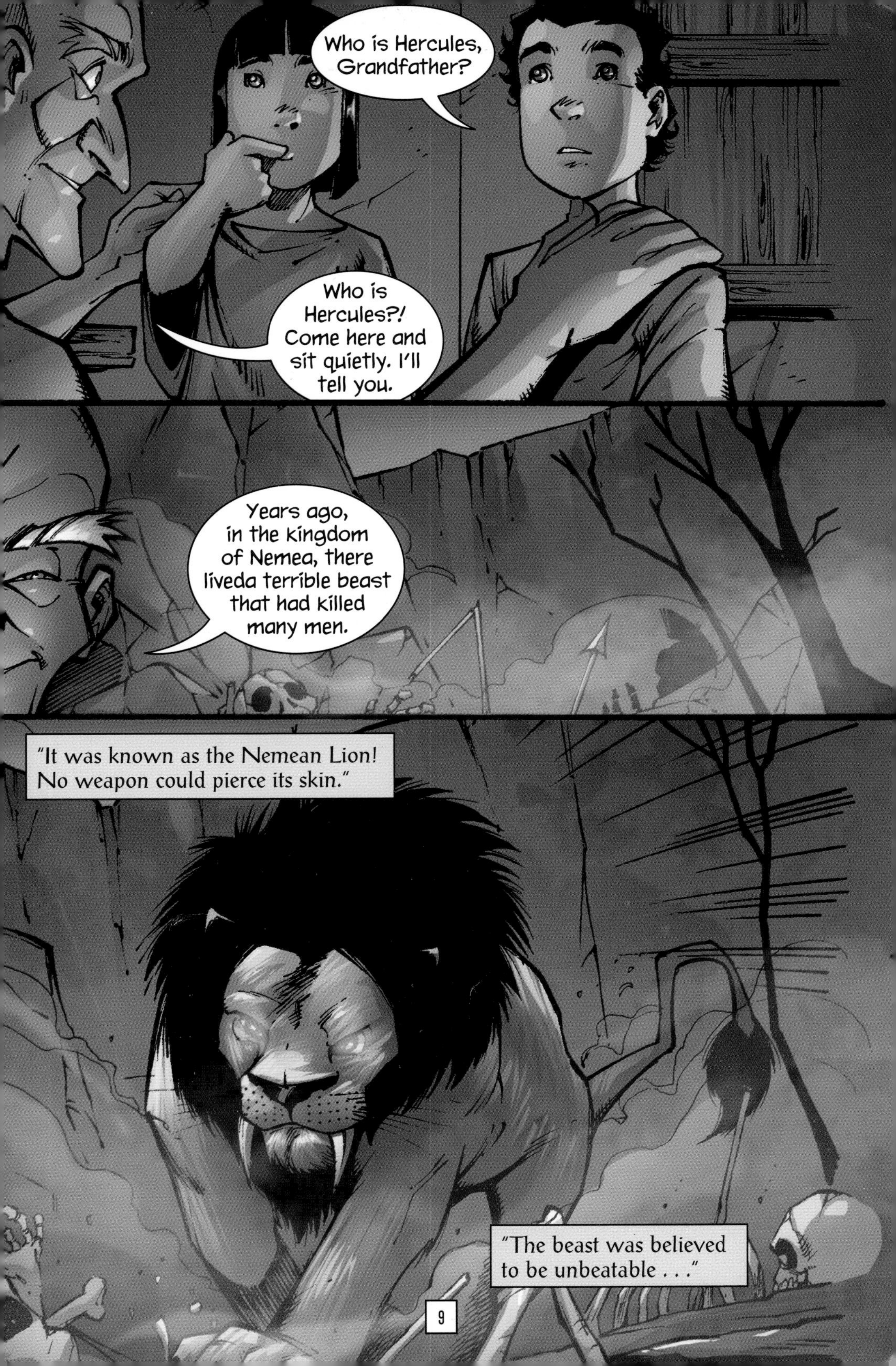
Who is Hercules, Grandfather?
Who is Hercules?! Come here and sit quietly. I'll tell you.
Years ago, in the kingdom of Nemea, there liveda terrible beast that had killed many men.
"It was known as the Nemean Lion! No weapon could pierce its skin."
"The beast was believed to be unbeatable . . ."

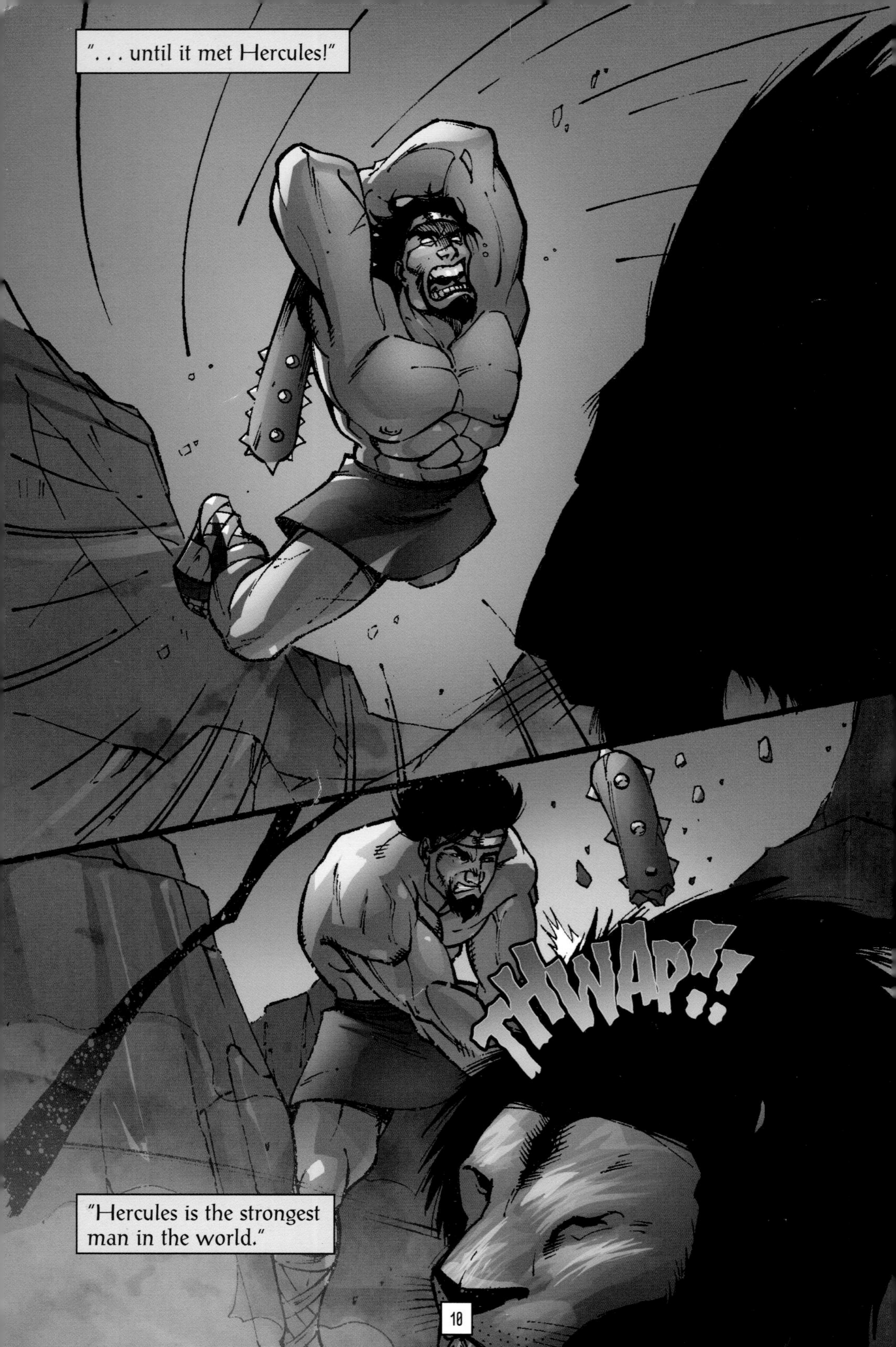
". . . until it met Hercules!"
THWAP!!
"Hercules is the strongest man in the world."

I knew I smelled a human nearby!
Our judgment will be swift and painful!
You know humans aren't allowed here, Pholus! This is our territory!
Brothers, you don't understand. This is Hercules, a former student of mine.
Believe me, I have nothing but respect for all centaurs.
And perhaps I can help you with your problem.
Problem? What problem?
The one charging right at you.

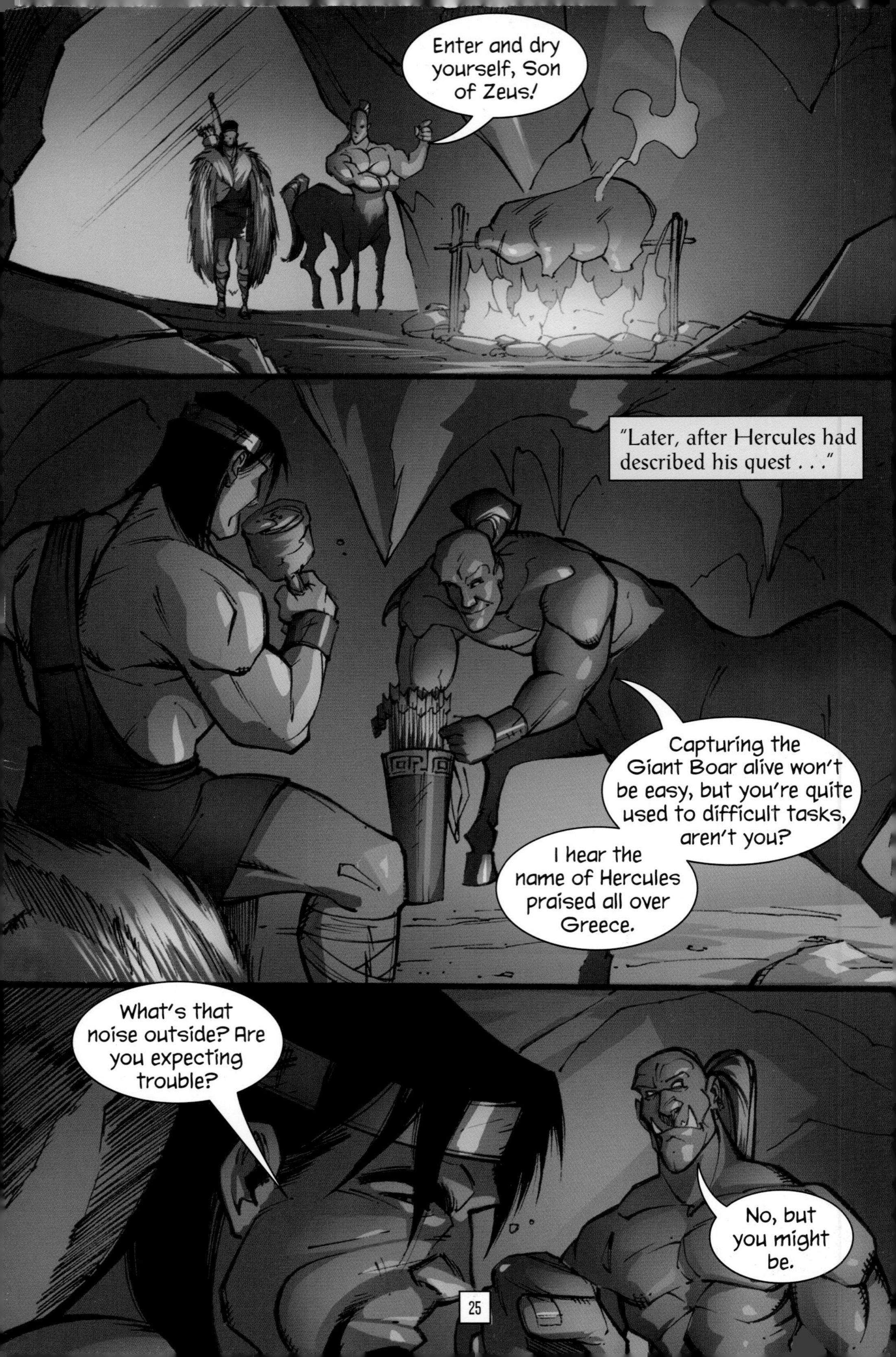
Enter and dry yourself, Son of Zeus!
"Later, after Hercules had described his quest . . ."
Capturing the Giant Boar alive won't be easy, but you're quite used to difficult tasks, aren't you?
I hear the name of Hercules praised all over Greece.
What's that noise outside? Are you expecting trouble?
No, but you might be.

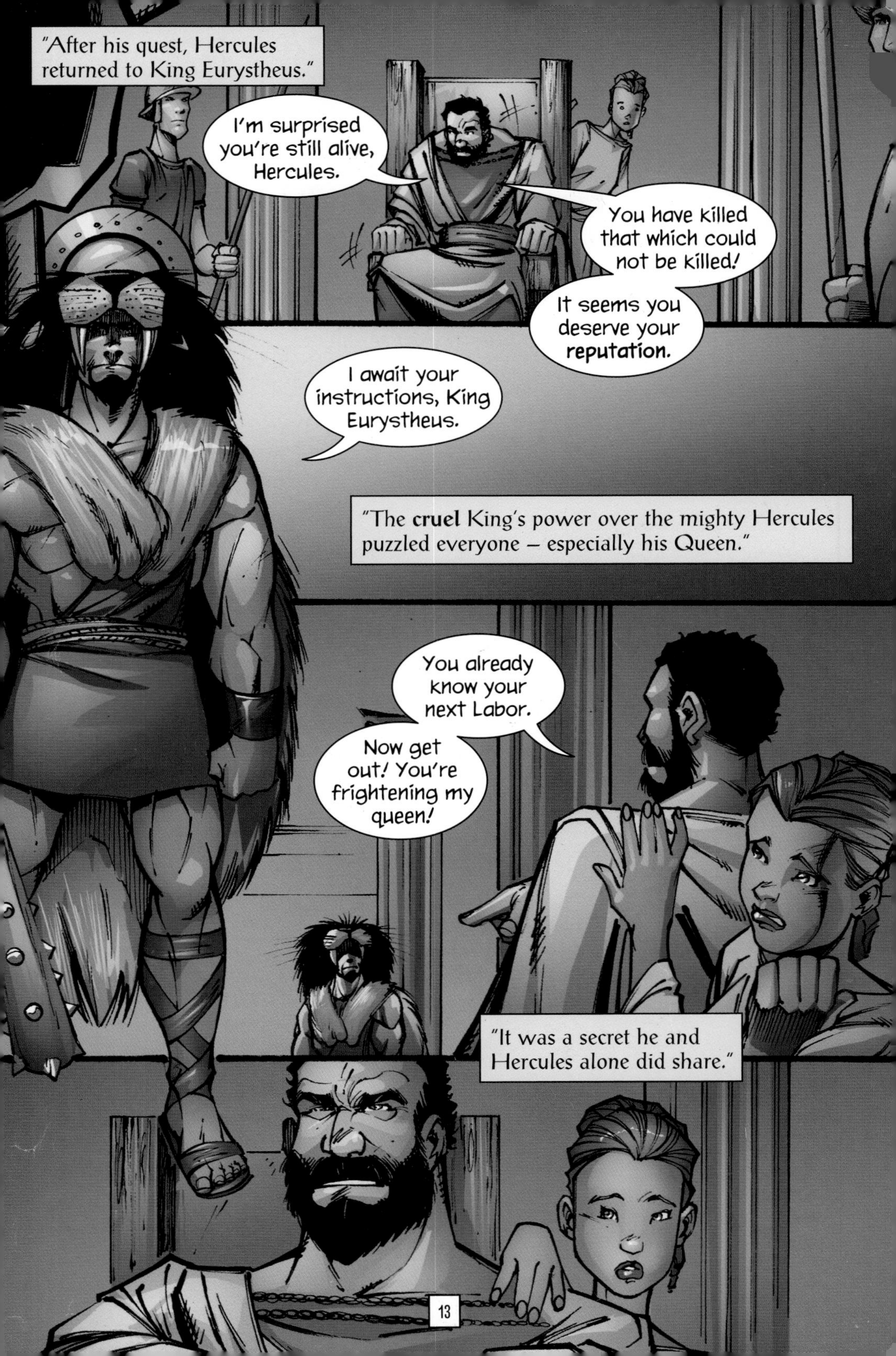
"After his quest, Hercules returned to King Eurystheus."
I'm surprised you're still alive, Hercules.
You have killed that which could not be killed!
It seems you deserve your **reputation**.
I await your instructions, King Eurystheus.
"The **cruel** King's power over the mighty Hercules puzzled everyone – especially his Queen."
You already know your next Labor.
Now get out! You're frightening my queen!
"It was a secret he and Hercules alone did share."

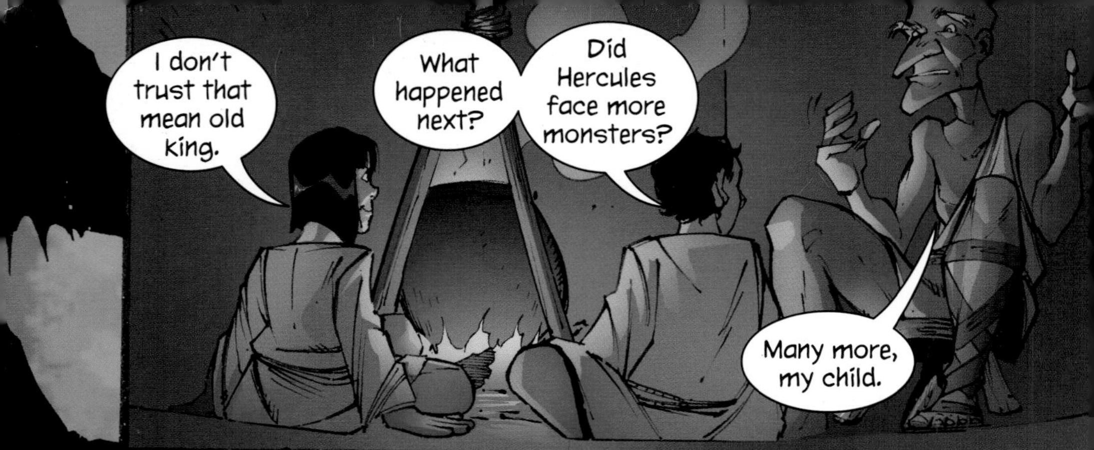
I don't trust that mean old king.
What happened next?
Did Hercules face more monsters?
Many more, my child.

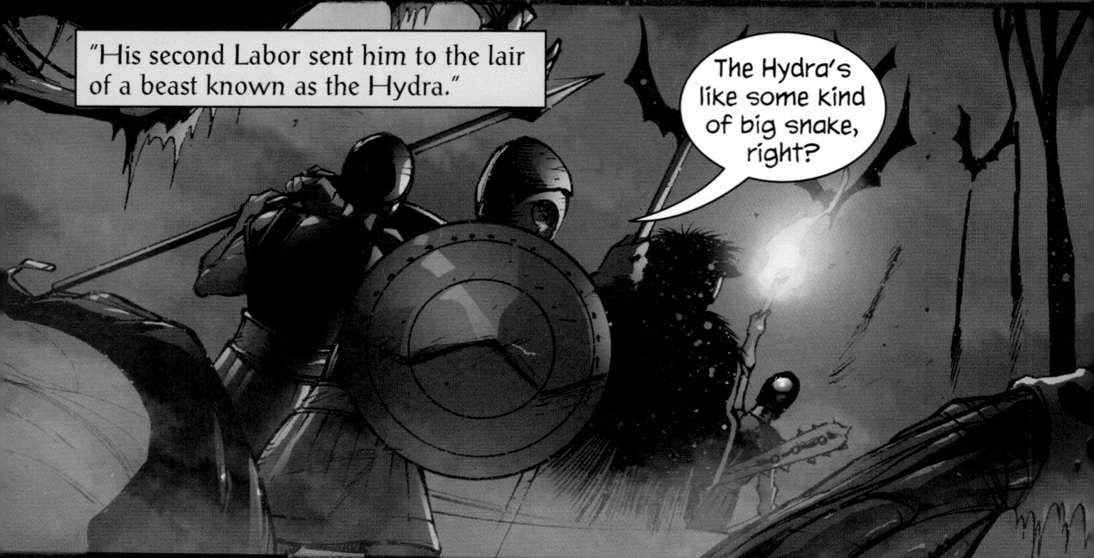
"His second Labor sent him to the lair of a beast known as the Hydra."
The Hydra's like some kind of big snake, right?

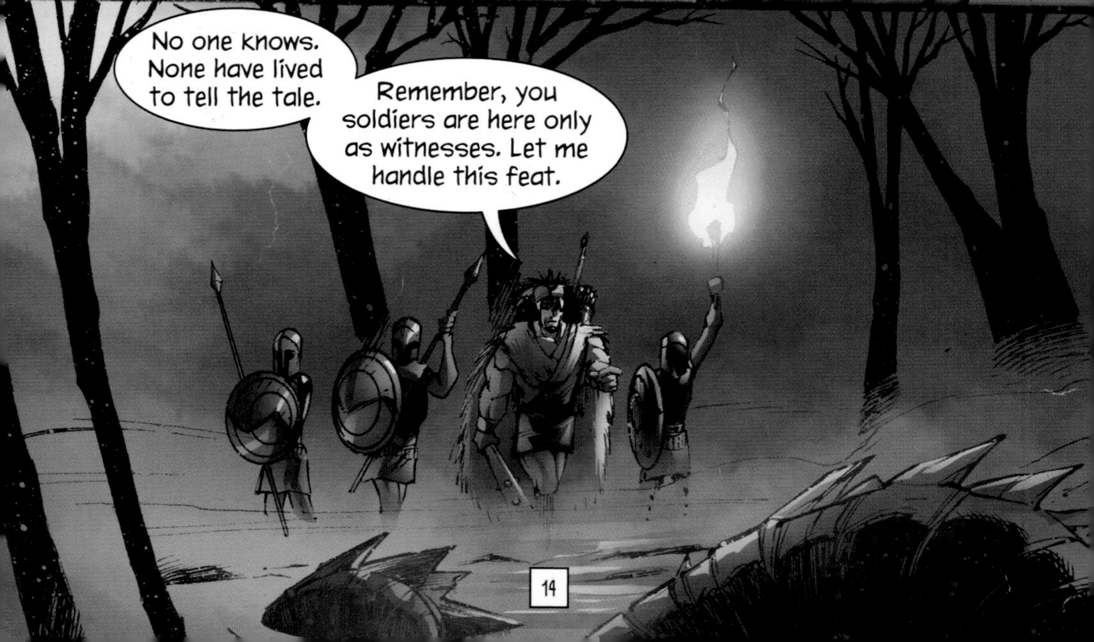
No one knows. None have lived to tell the tale.
Remember, you soldiers are here only as witnesses. Let me handle this feat.

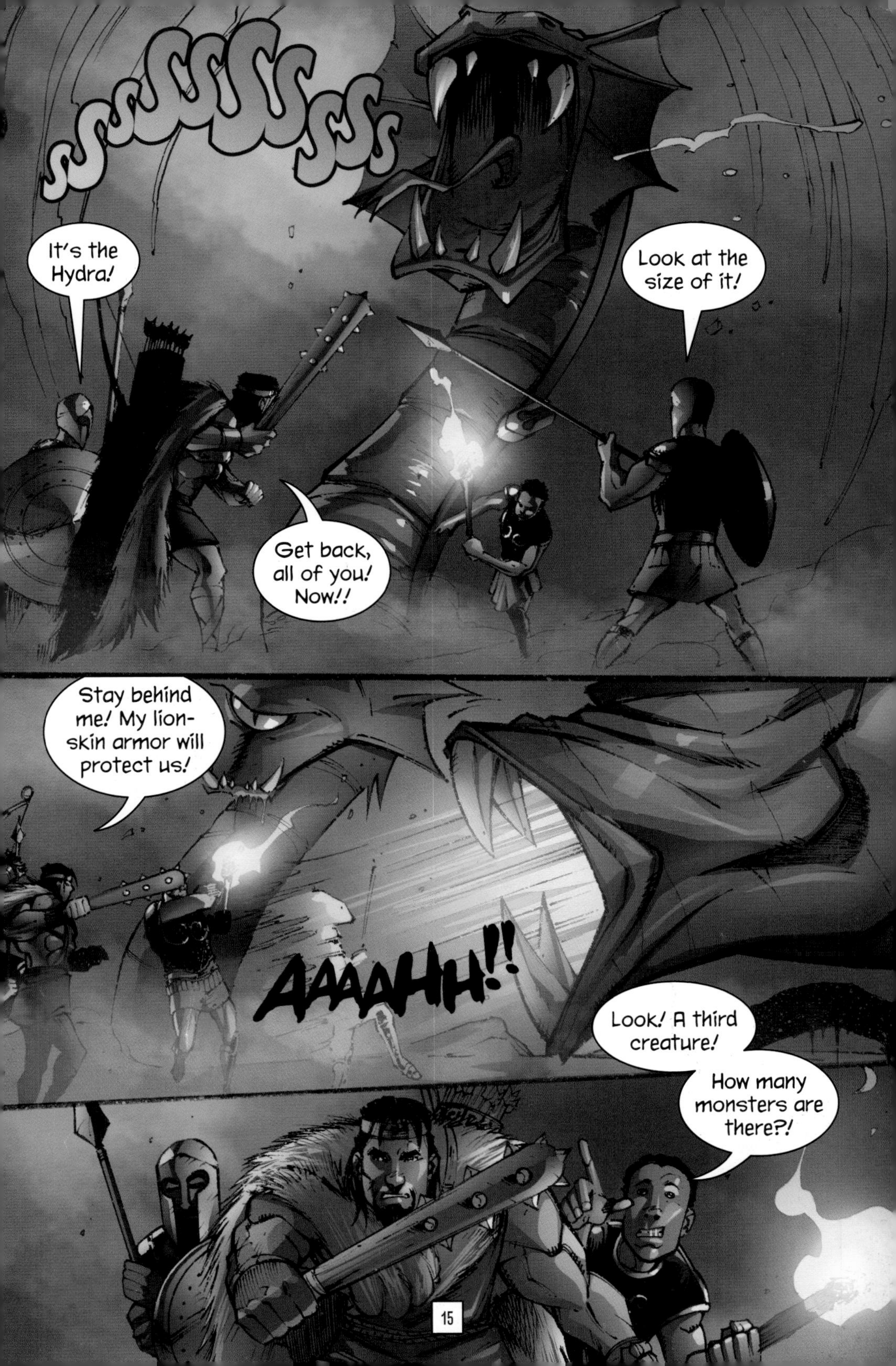
SSSSSSSSSS
It's the Hydra!
Look at the size of it!
Get back, all of you! Now!!
Stay behind me! My lion-skin armor will protect us!
AAAAHH!!
Look! A third creature!
How many monsters are there?!

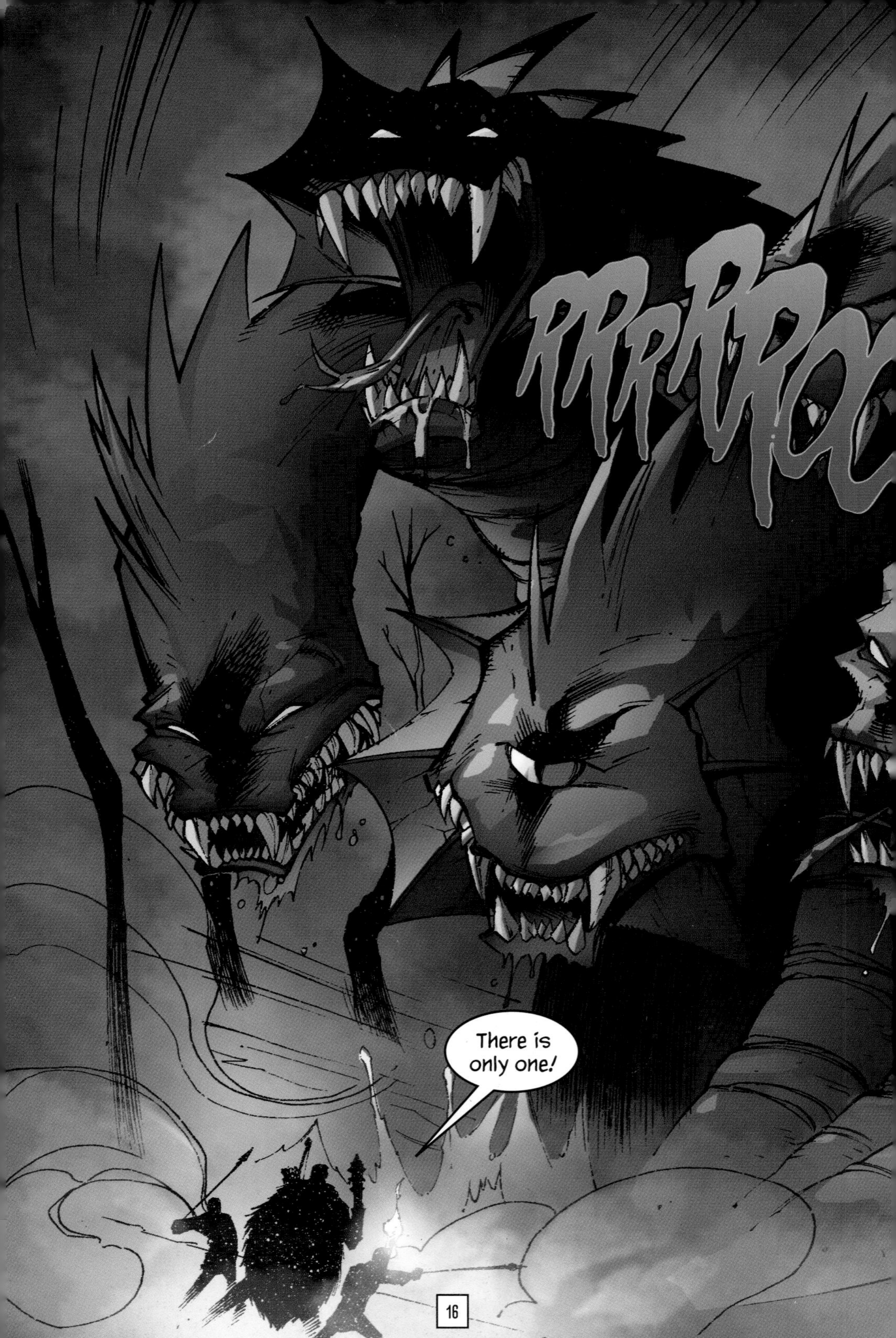
RRRRROO
There is only one!

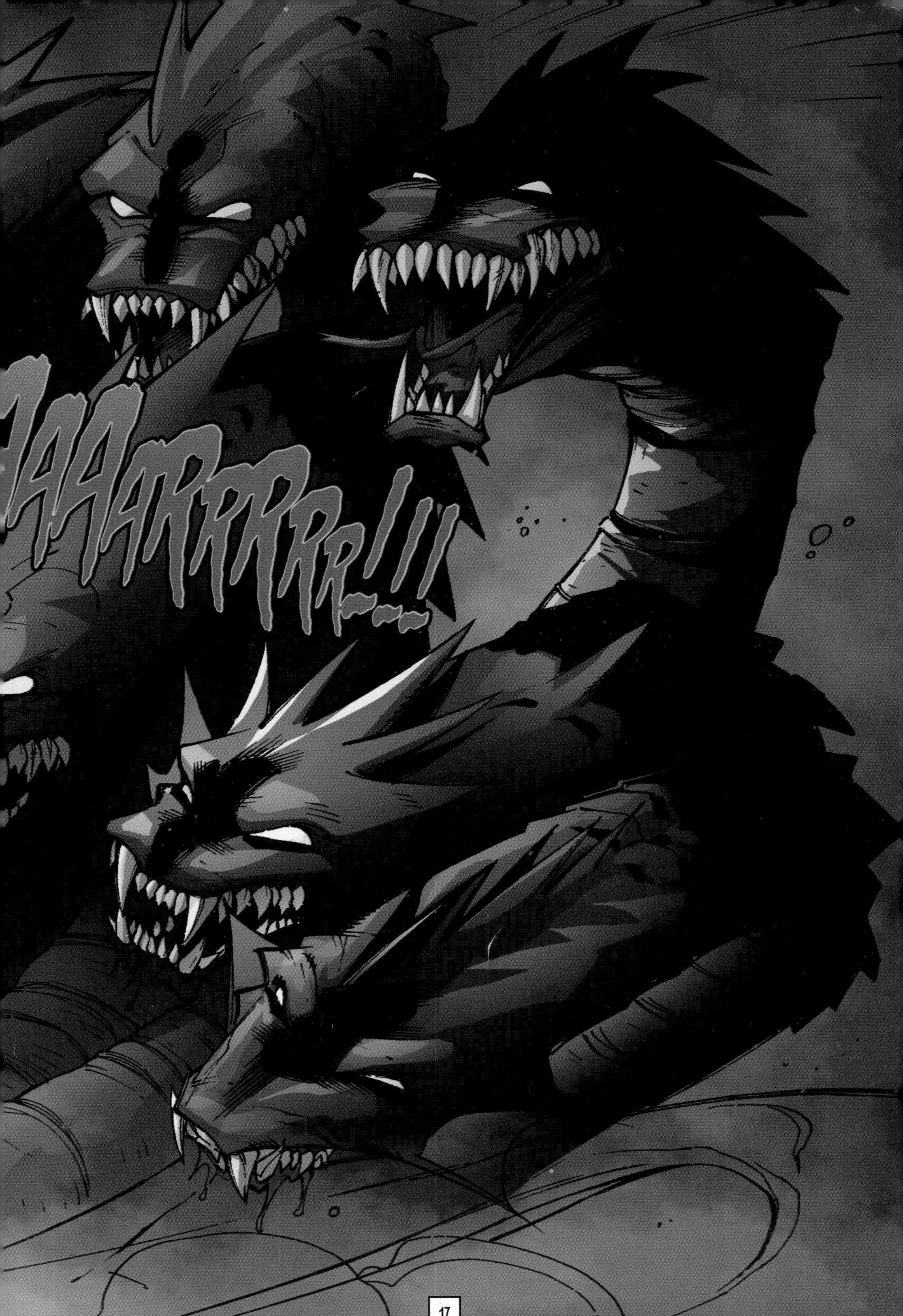
AAAARRRRR!!!

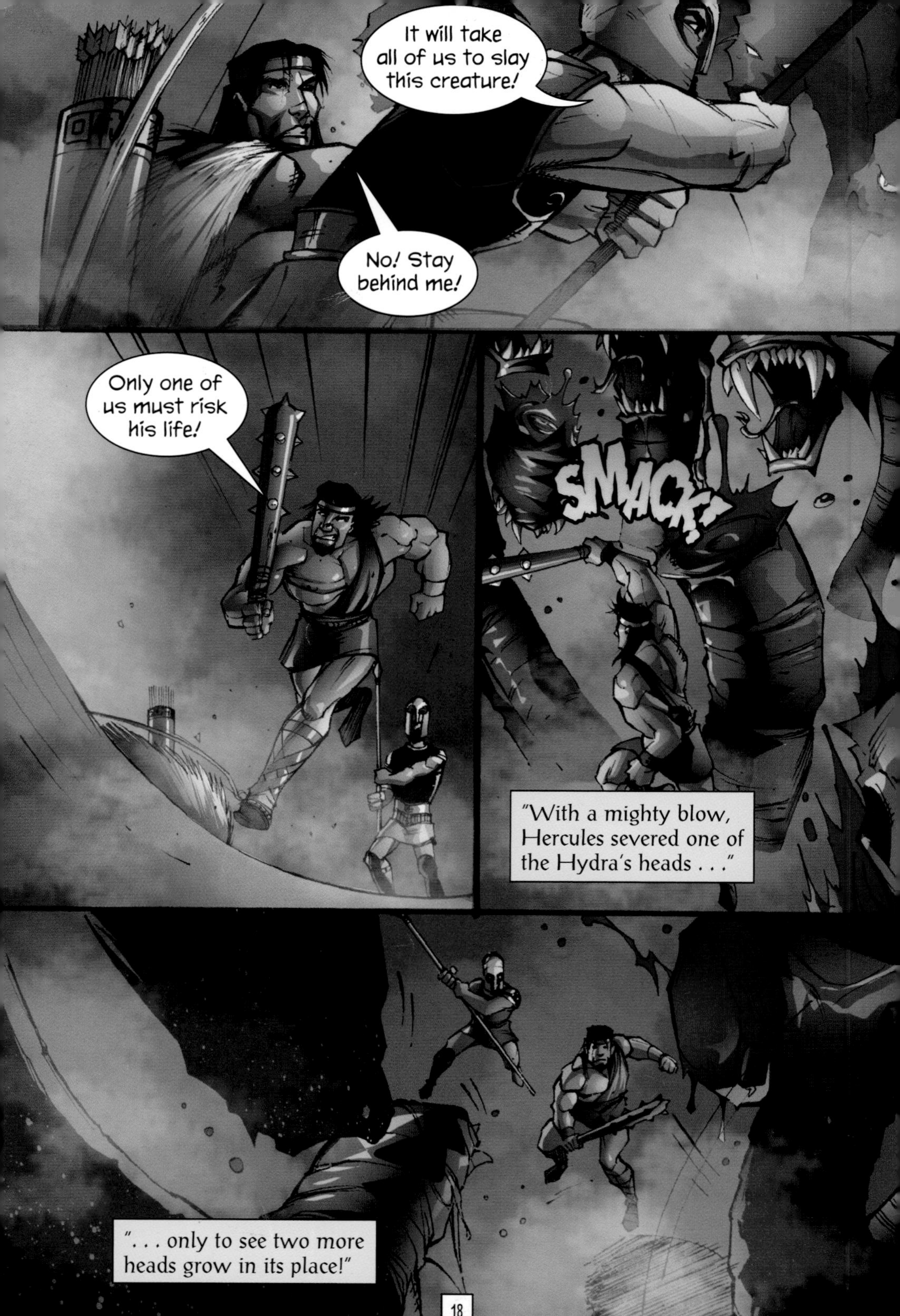
It will take all of us to slay this creature!
No! Stay behind me!
Only one of us must risk his life!
SMACK!
"With a mighty blow, Hercules severed one of the Hydra's heads . . ."
". . . only to see two more heads grow in its place!"

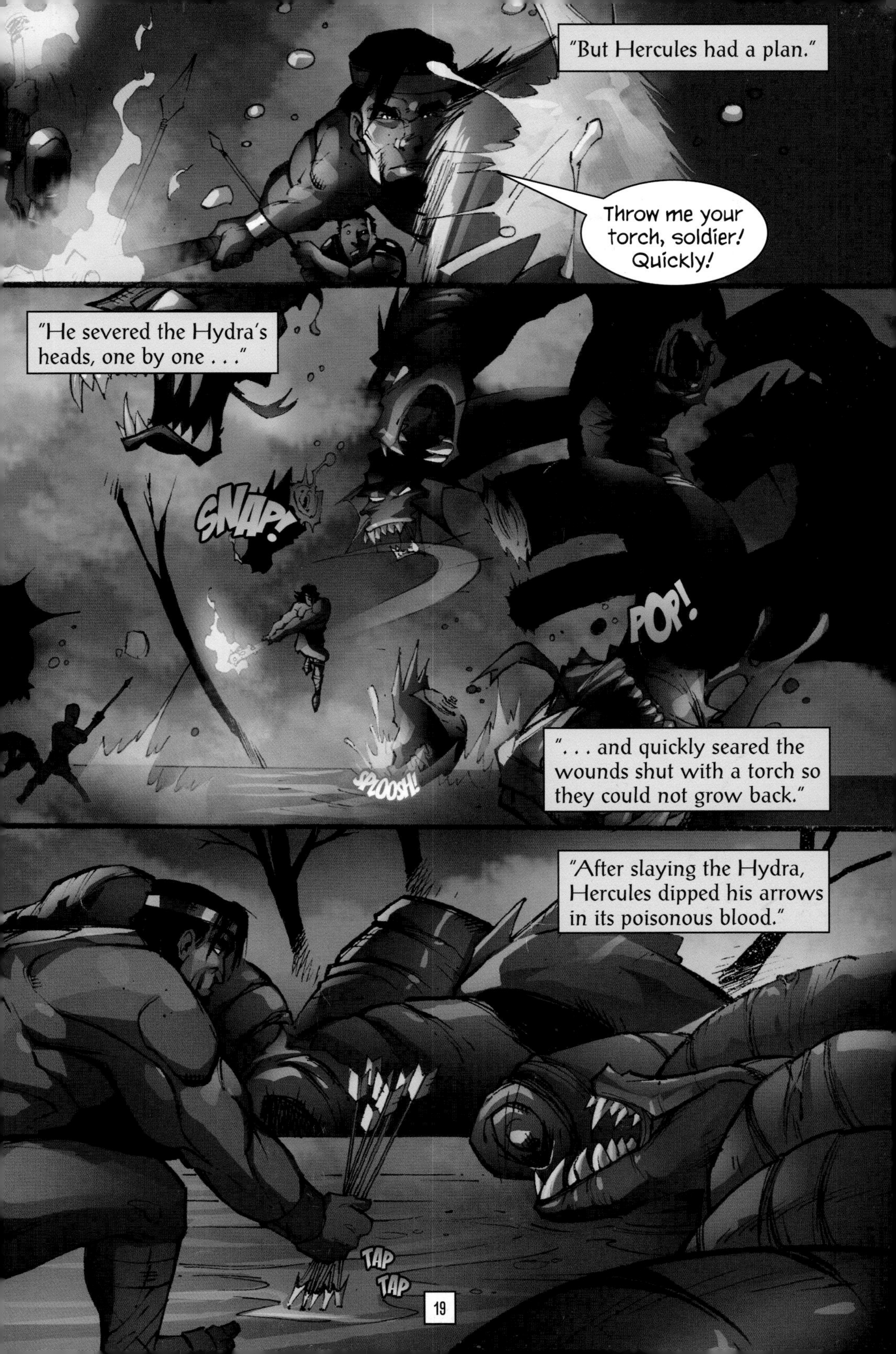
"But Hercules had a plan."
Throw me your torch, soldier! Quickly!
"He severed the Hydra's heads, one by one . . ."
SNAP!
POP!
SPLOOSH!
". . . and quickly seared the wounds shut with a torch so they could not grow back."
"After slaying the Hydra, Hercules dipped his arrows in its poisonous blood."
TAP
TAP

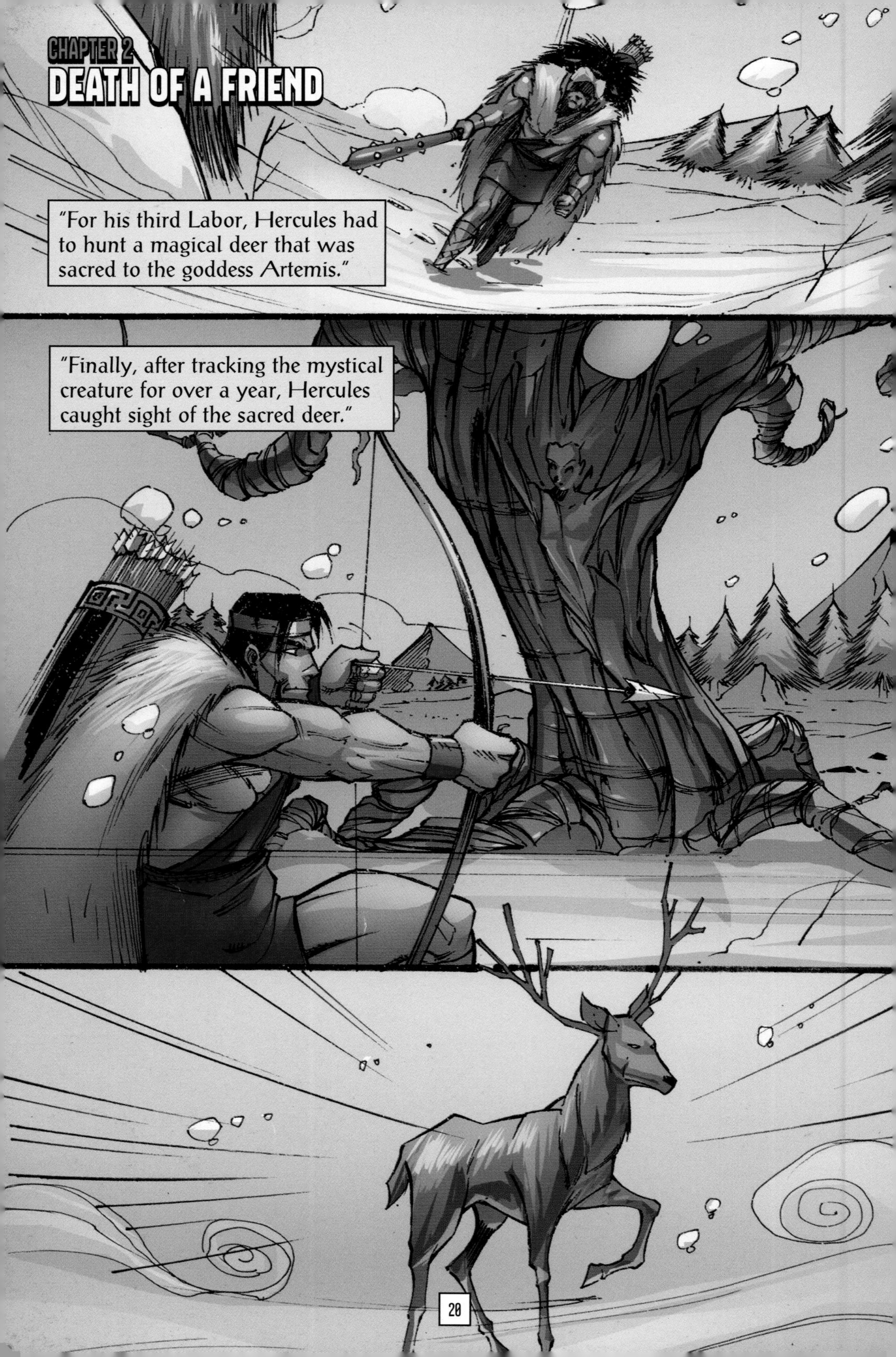
CHAPTER 2
DEATH OF A FRIEND
"For his third Labor, Hercules had to hunt a magical deer that was sacred to the goddess Artemis."
"Finally, after tracking the mystical creature for over a year, Hercules caught sight of the sacred deer."

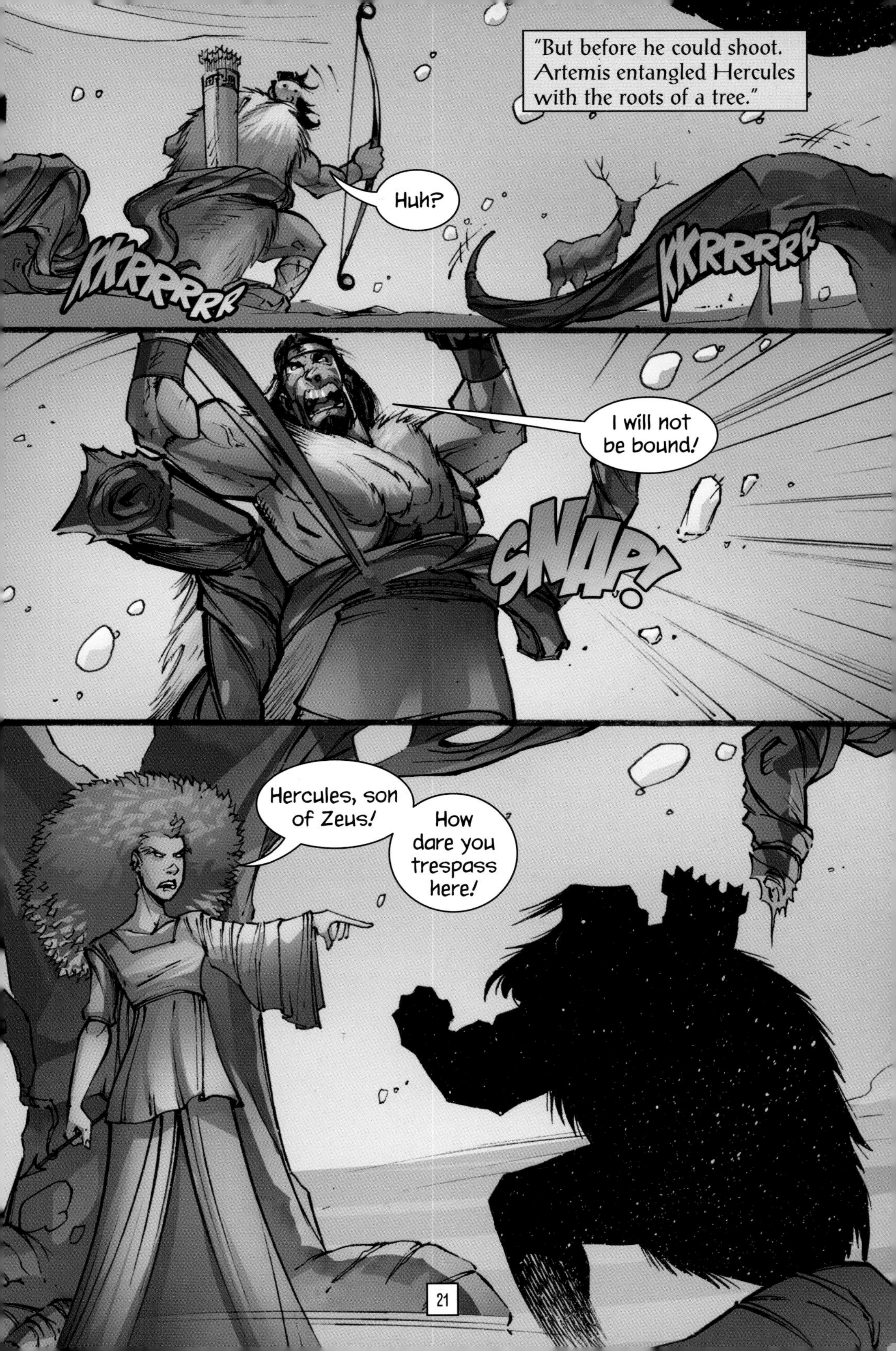
"But before he could shoot. Artemis entangled Hercules with the roots of a tree."
Huh?
KKRRRRR
KKRRRRR
I will not be bound!
SNAP!
Hercules, son of Zeus!
How dare you trespass here!

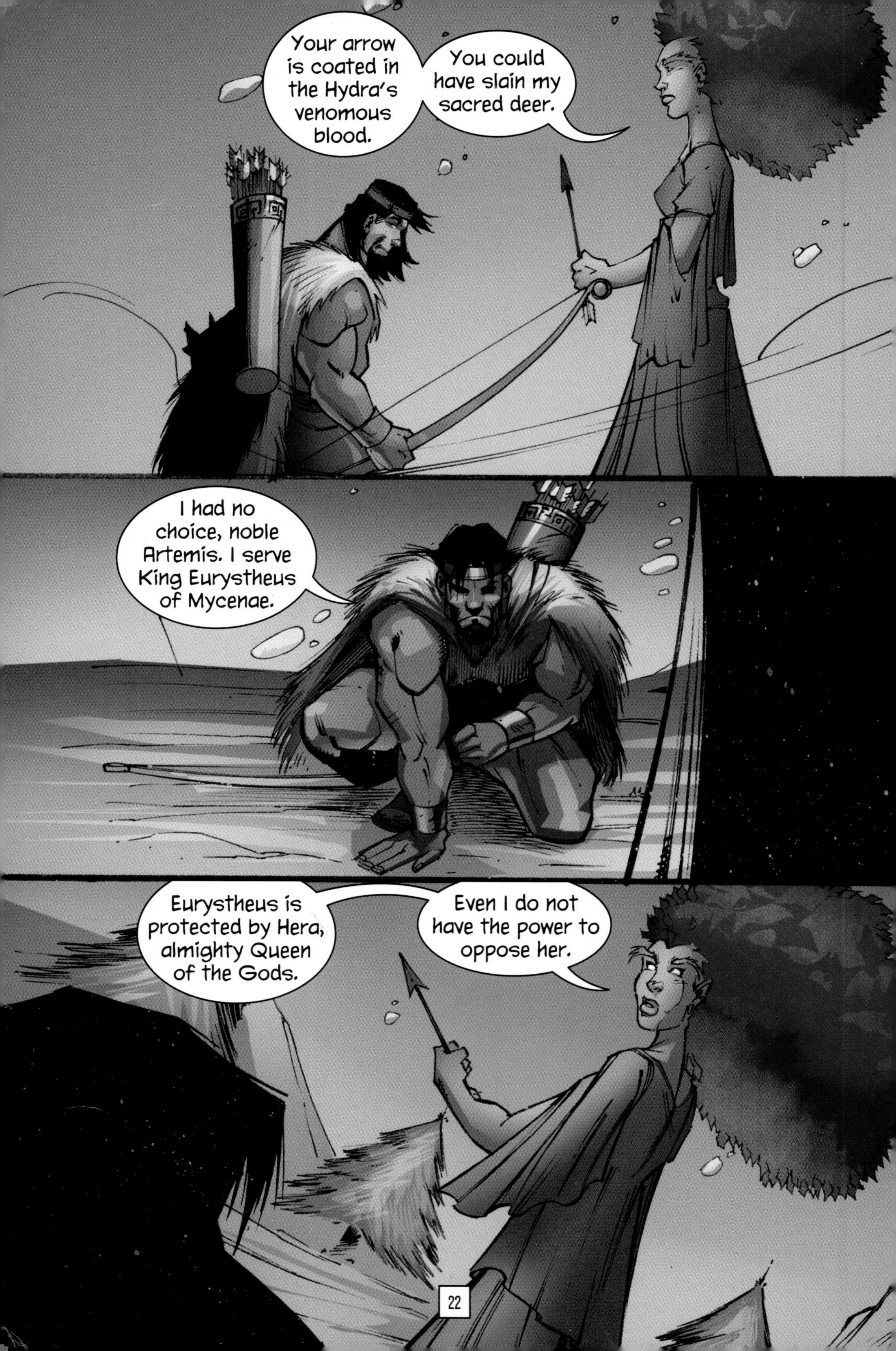
Your arrow is coated in the Hydra's venomous blood.
You could have slain my sacred deer.
I had no choice, noble Artemis. I serve King Eurystheus of Mycenae.
Eurystheus is protected by Hera, almighty Queen of the Gods.
Even I do not have the power to oppose her.

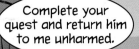

My pet will follow you, Hercules.

Complete your quest and return him to me unharmed.

Hercules brought the magic deer to the King. Eurystheus became furious at the hero's triumph.

Why did Hercules serve that evil king, Grandfather?

Patience, child. All will be revealed.

But first, the fourth Labor of Hercules . . .

The hunt for the Giant Boar of Mount Erymanthus!

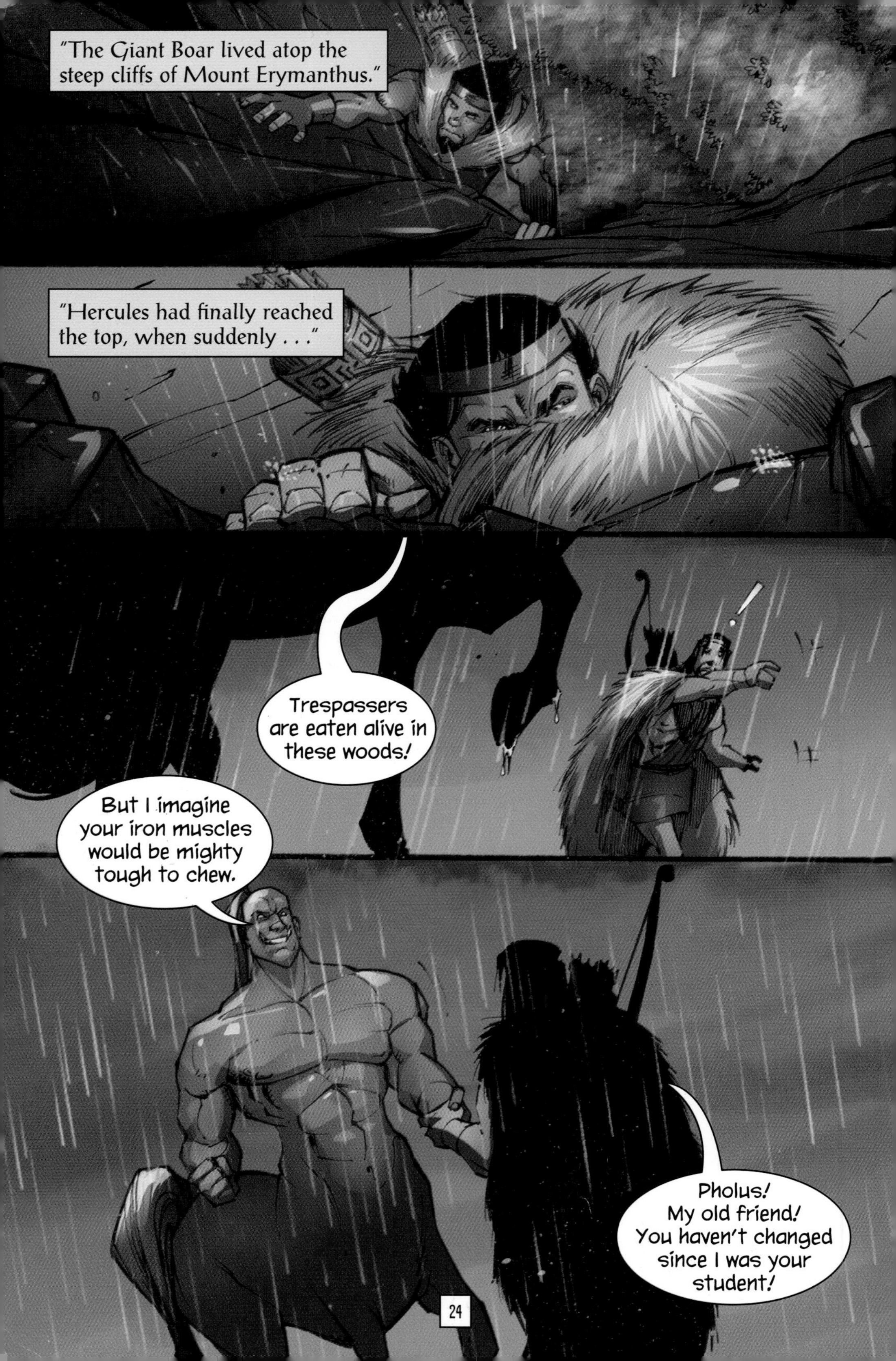
"The Giant Boar lived atop the steep cliffs of Mount Erymanthus."
"Hercules had finally reached the top, when suddenly . . ."
Trespassers are eaten alive in these woods!
!
But I imagine your iron muscles would be mighty tough to chew.
Pholus! My old friend! You haven't changed since I was your student!

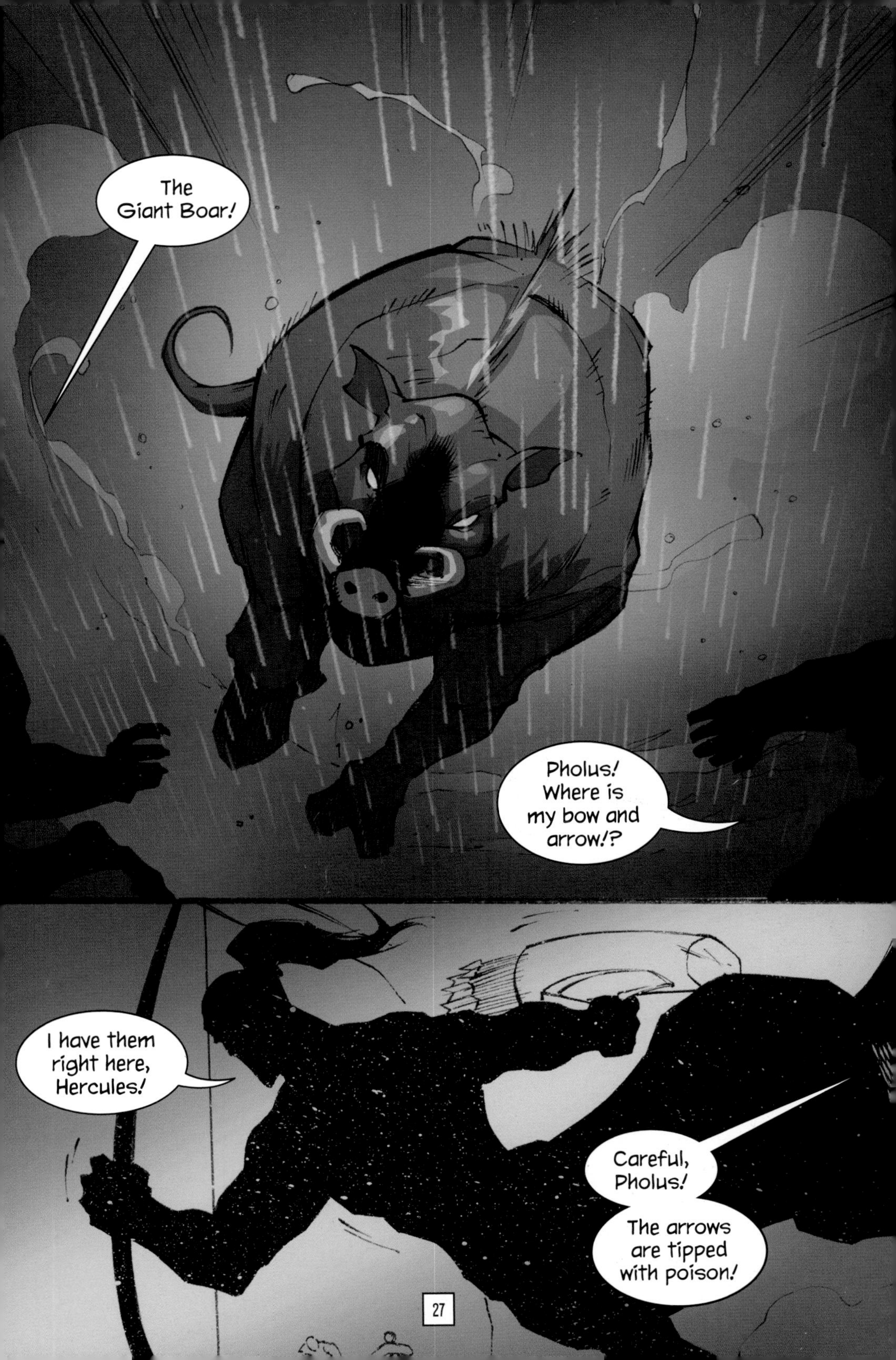
The Giant Boar!
Pholus! Where is my bow and arrow!?
I have them right here, Hercules!
Careful, Pholus!
The arrows are tipped with poison!

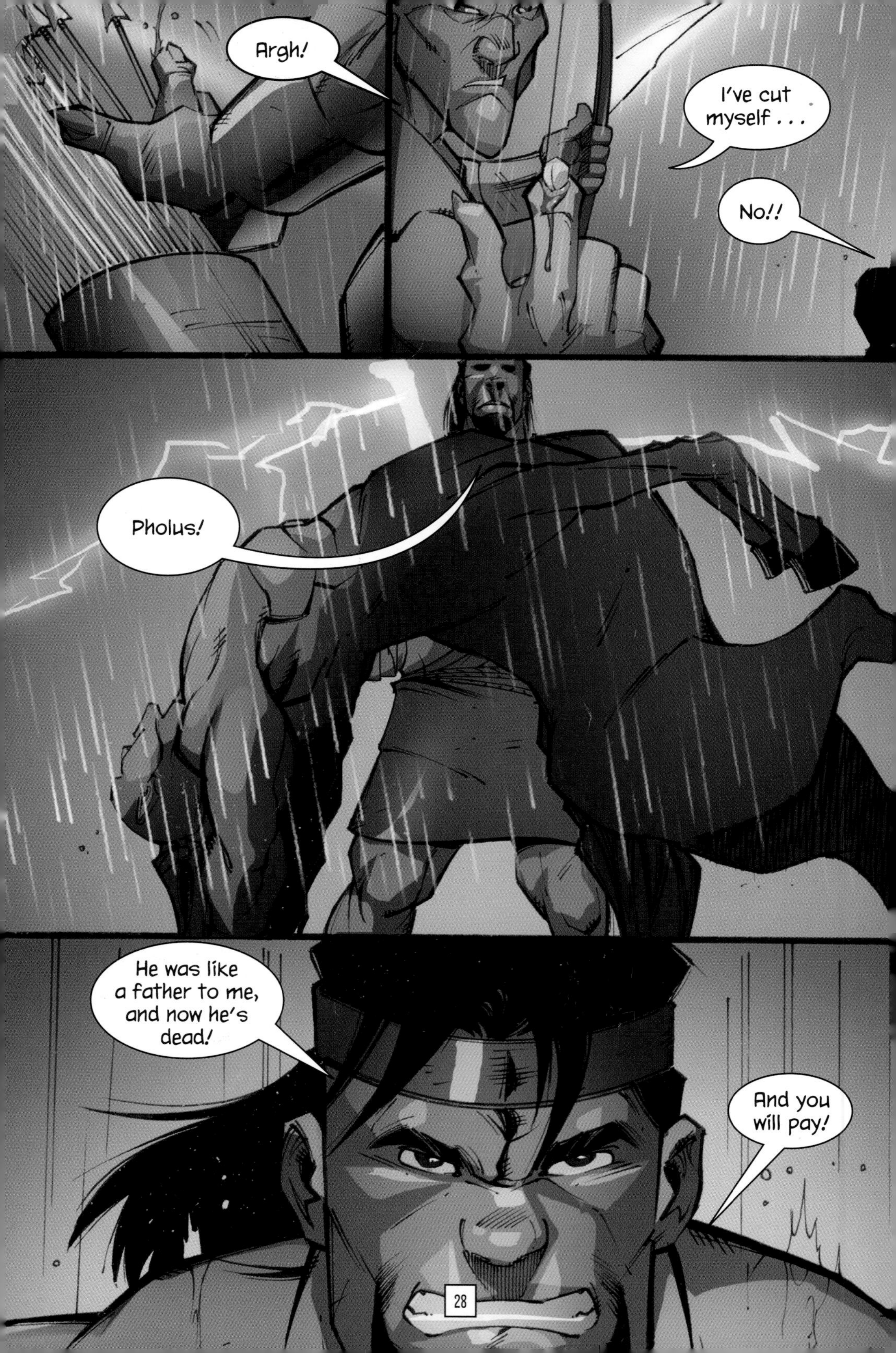
Argh!
I've cut myself . . .
No!!
Pholus!
He was like a father to me, and now he's dead!
And you will pay!

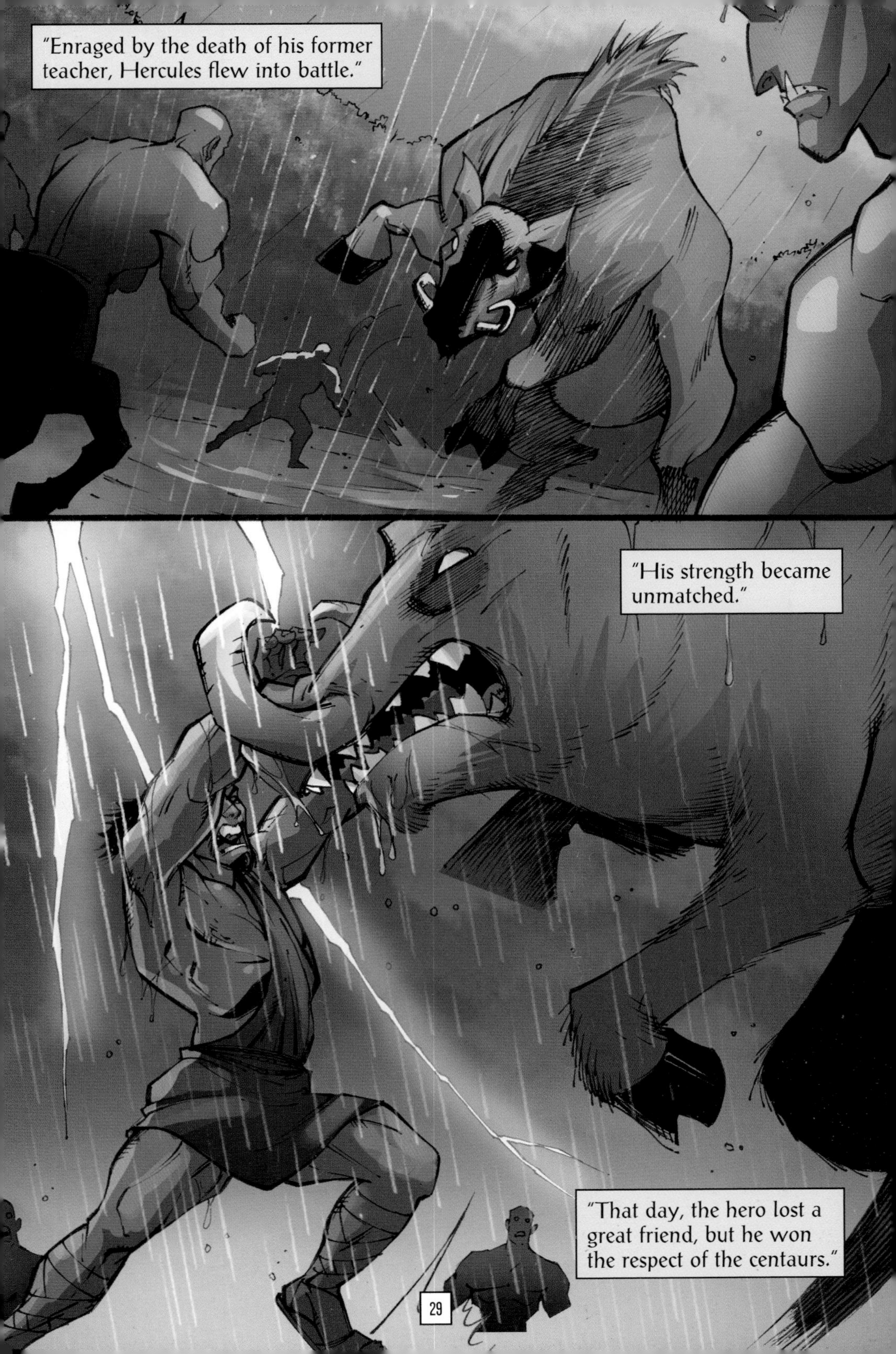
"Enraged by the death of his former teacher, Hercules flew into battle."
"His strength became unmatched."
"That day, the hero lost a great friend, but he won the respect of the centaurs."

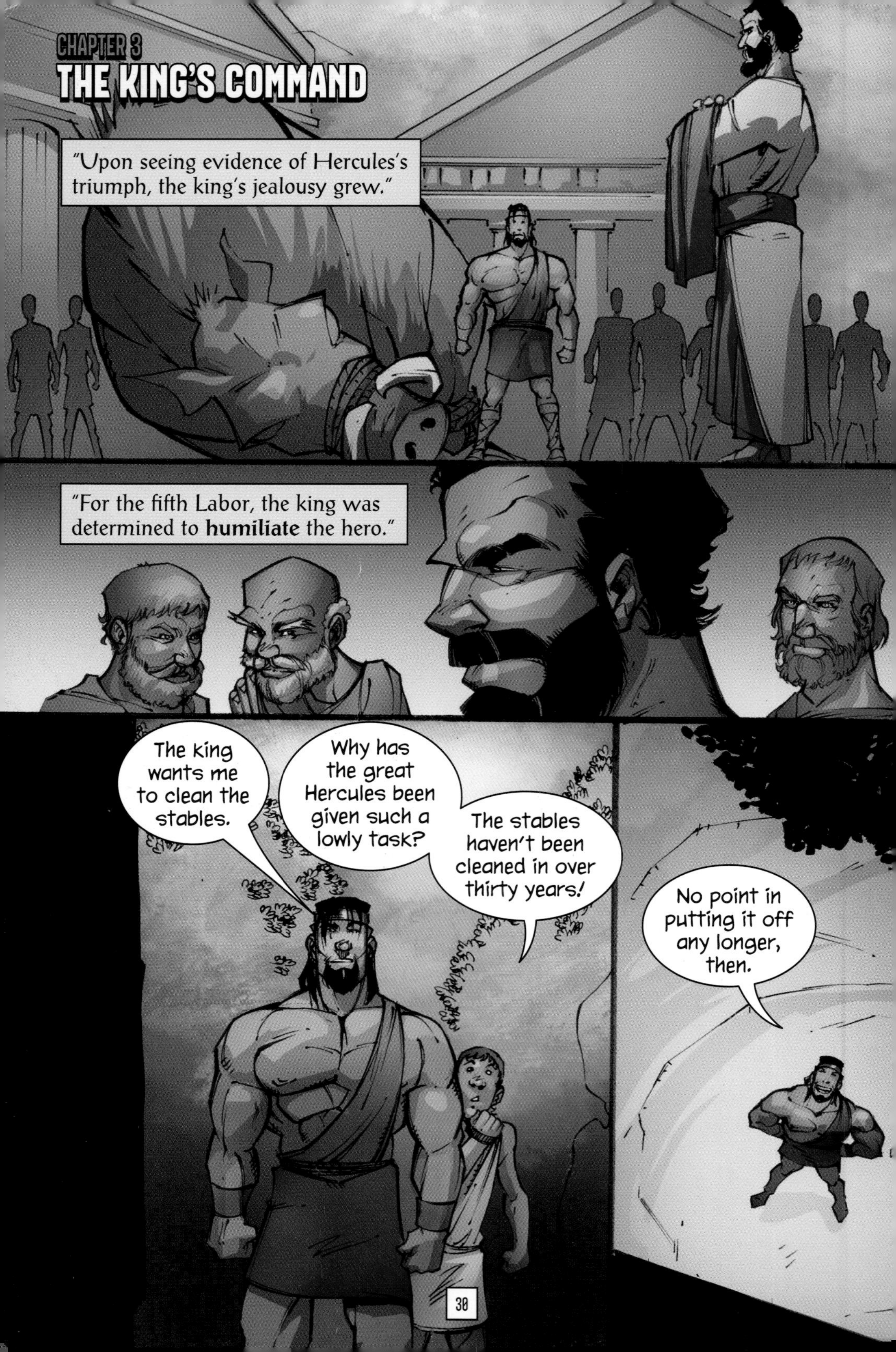
CHAPTER 3
THE KING'S COMMAND
"Upon seeing evidence of Hercules's triumph, the king's jealousy grew."
"For the fifth Labor, the king was determined to **humiliate** the hero."
The king wants me to clean the stables.
Why has the great Hercules been given such a lowly task?
The stables haven't been cleaned in over thirty years!
No point in putting it off any longer, then.

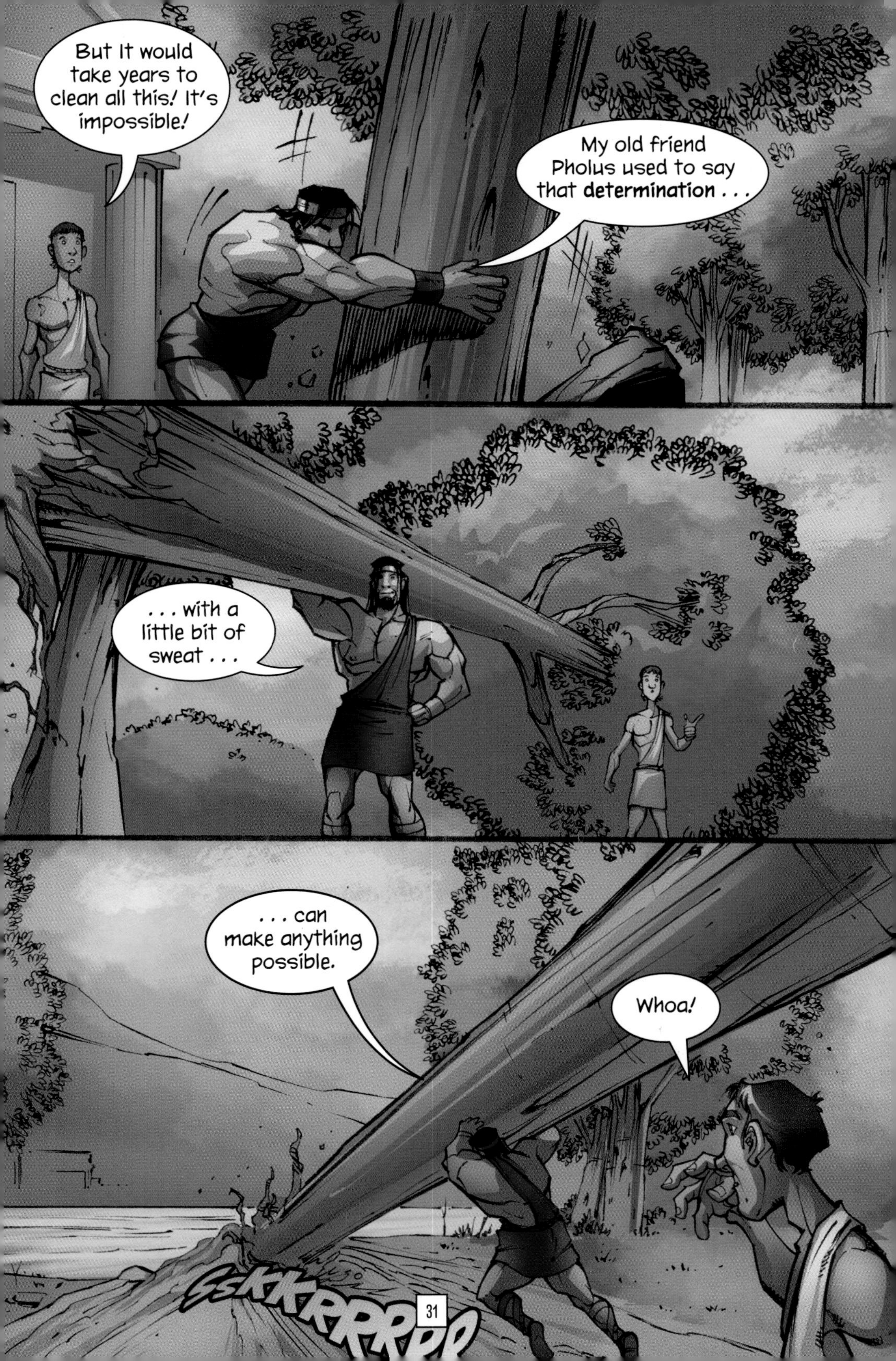
But it would take years to clean all this! It's impossible!
My old friend Pholus used to say that determination . . .
. . . with a little bit of sweat . . .
. . . can make anything possible.
Whoa!
SSKKRRRRR

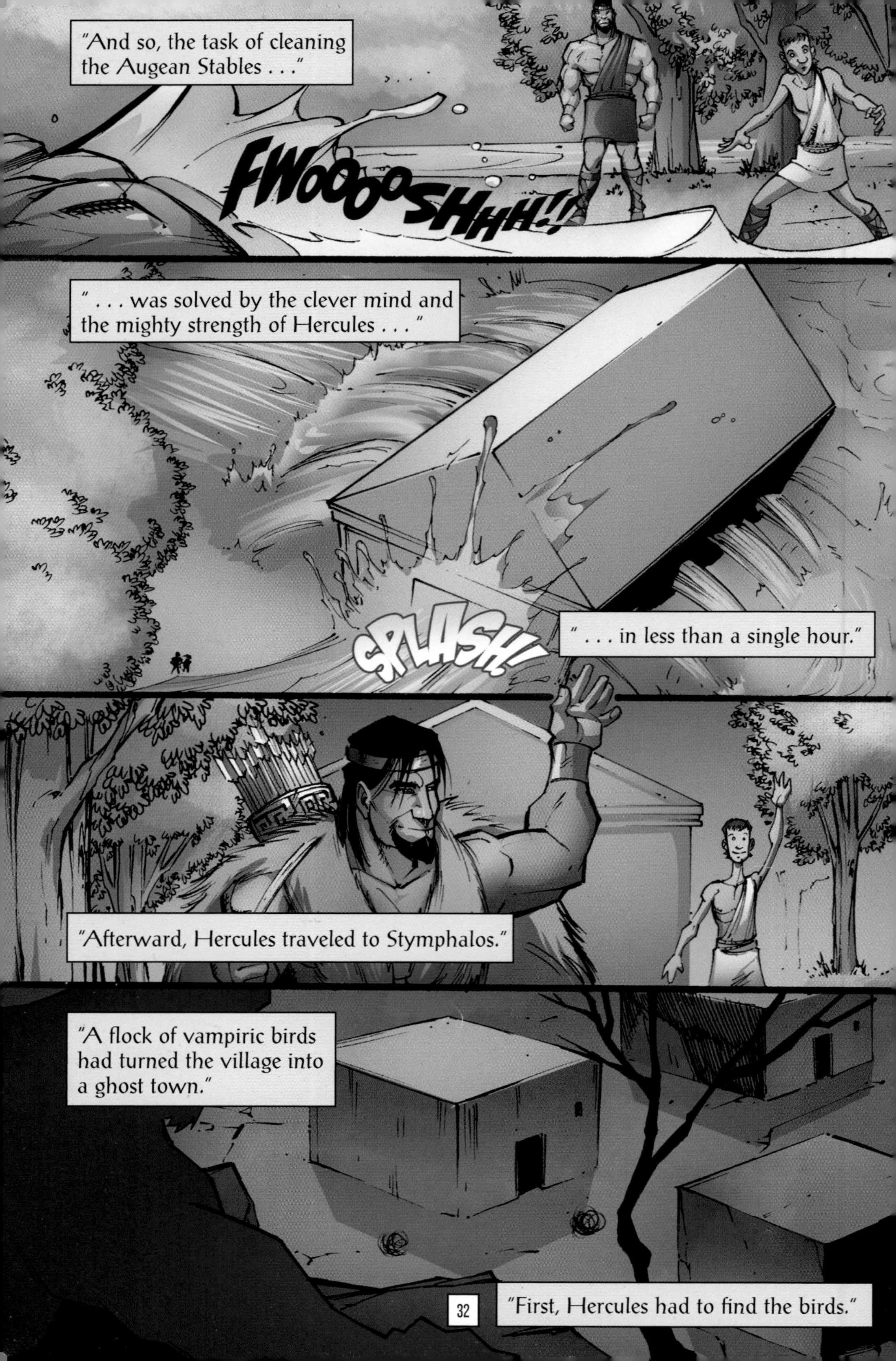
"And so, the task of cleaning the Augean Stables . . ."
FWOOOOSHHH!!
" . . . was solved by the clever mind and the mighty strength of Hercules . . . "
SPLASH!
" . . . in less than a single hour."
"Afterward, Hercules traveled to Stymphalos."
"A flock of vampiric birds had turned the village into a ghost town."
"First, Hercules had to find the birds."

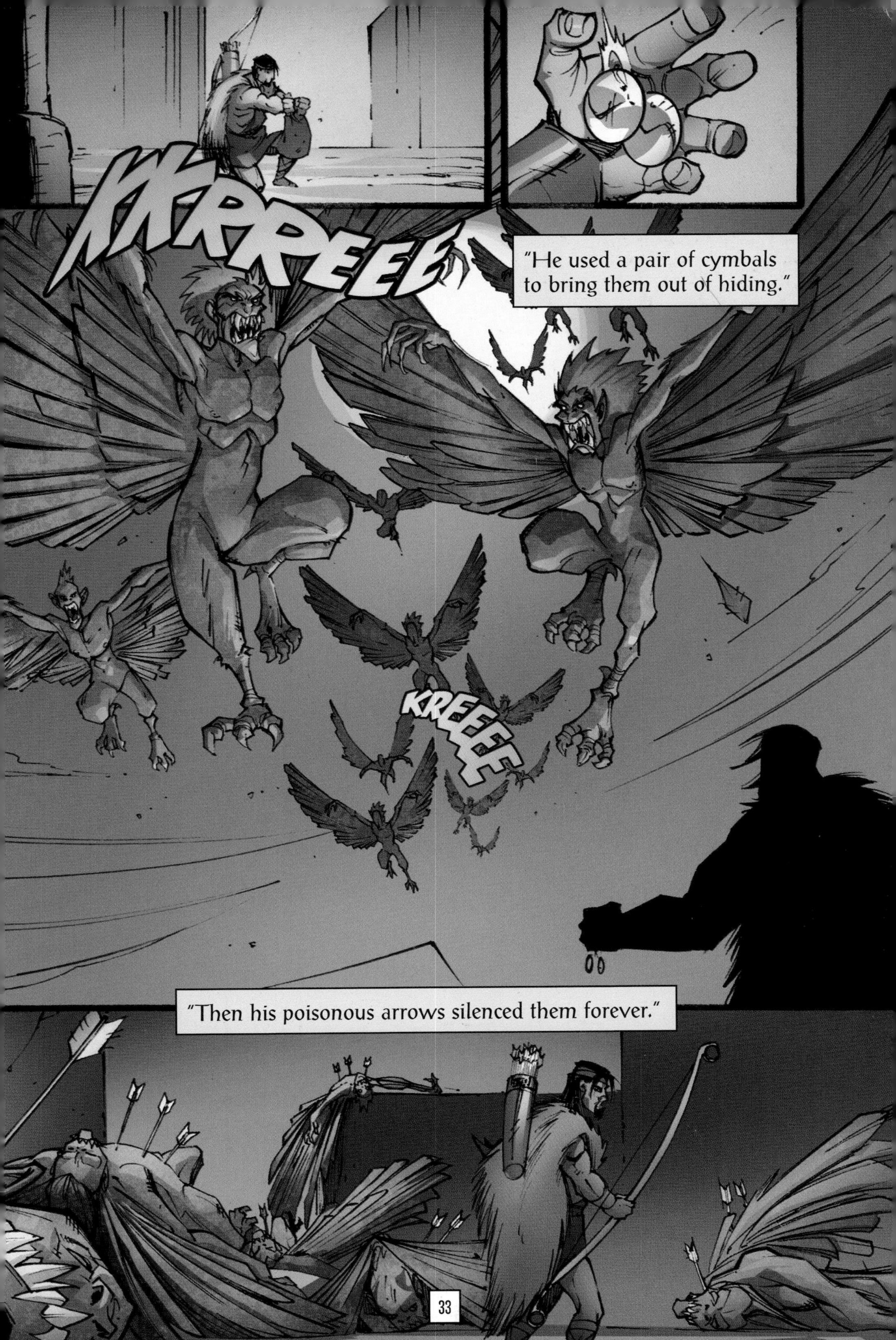
KKRREEE
"He used a pair of cymbals to bring them out of hiding."
KREEEE
"Then his poisonous arrows silenced them forever."

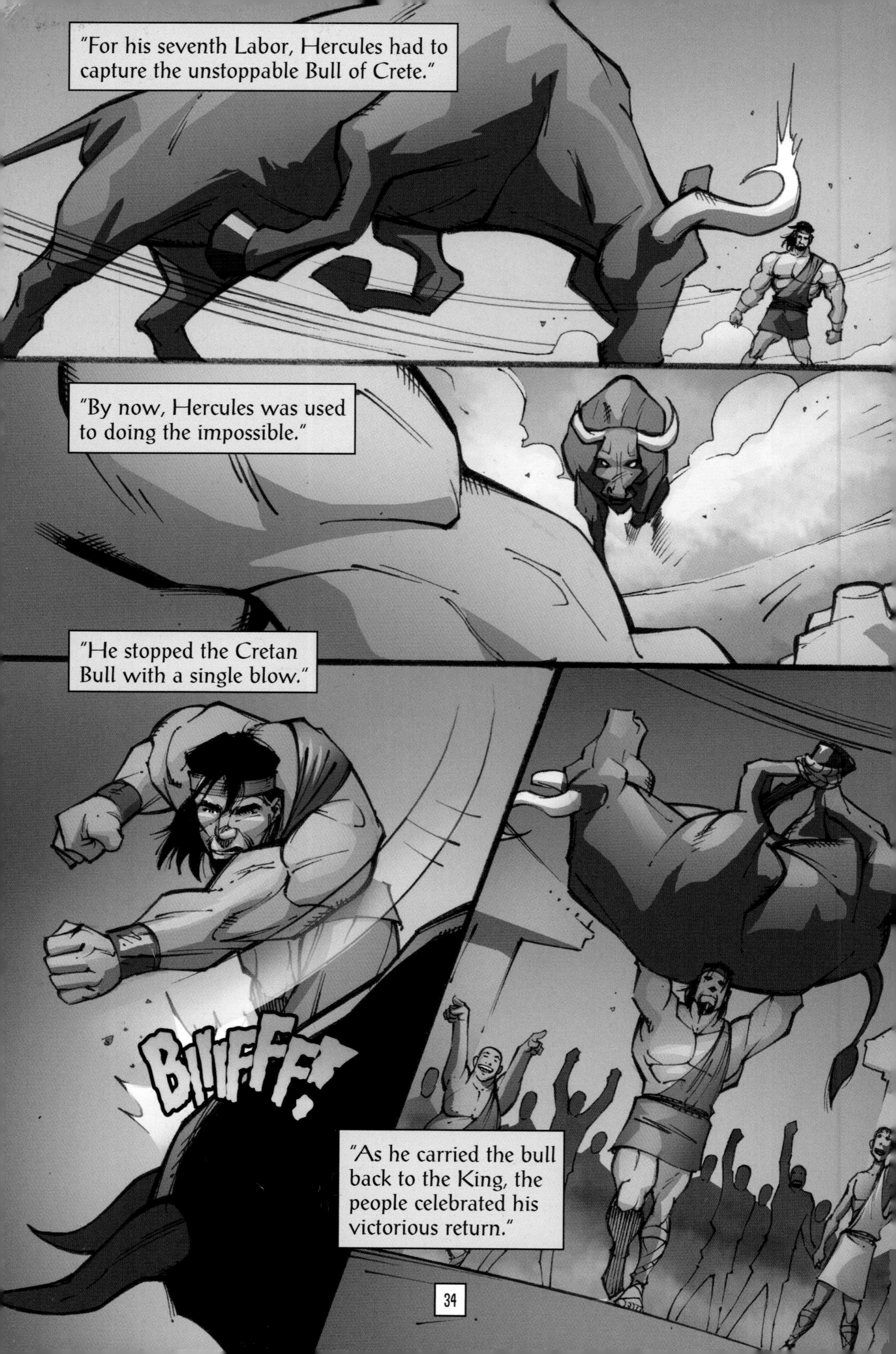
"For his seventh Labor, Hercules had to capture the unstoppable Bull of Crete."
"By now, Hercules was used to doing the impossible."
"He stopped the Cretan Bull with a single blow."
BIIIFFF!
"As he carried the bull back to the King, the people celebrated his victorious return."

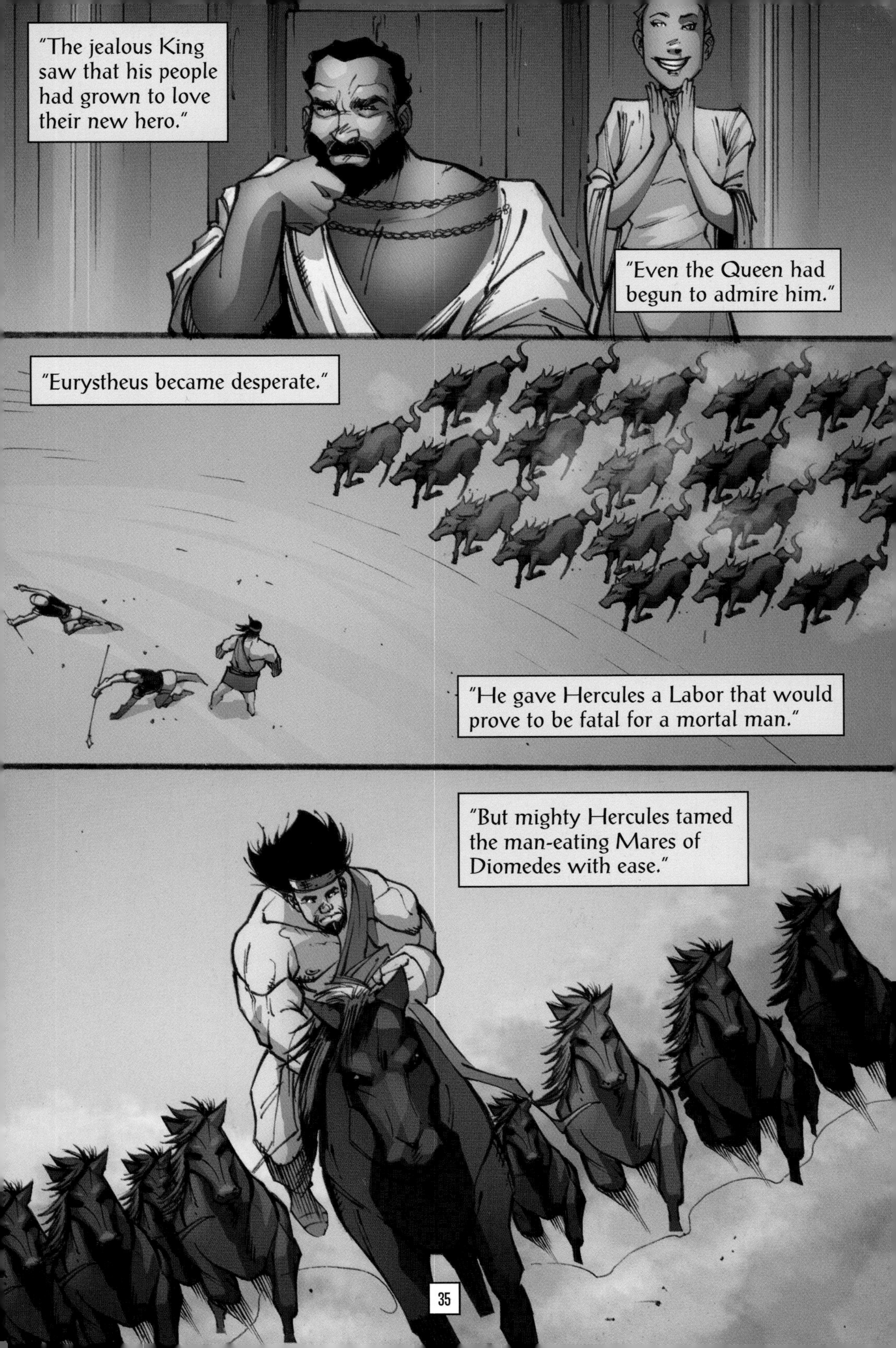
"The jealous King saw that his people had grown to love their new hero."
"Even the Queen had begun to admire him."
"Eurystheus became desperate."
"He gave Hercules a Labor that would prove to be fatal for a mortal man."
"But mighty Hercules tamed the man-eating Mares of Diomedes with ease."

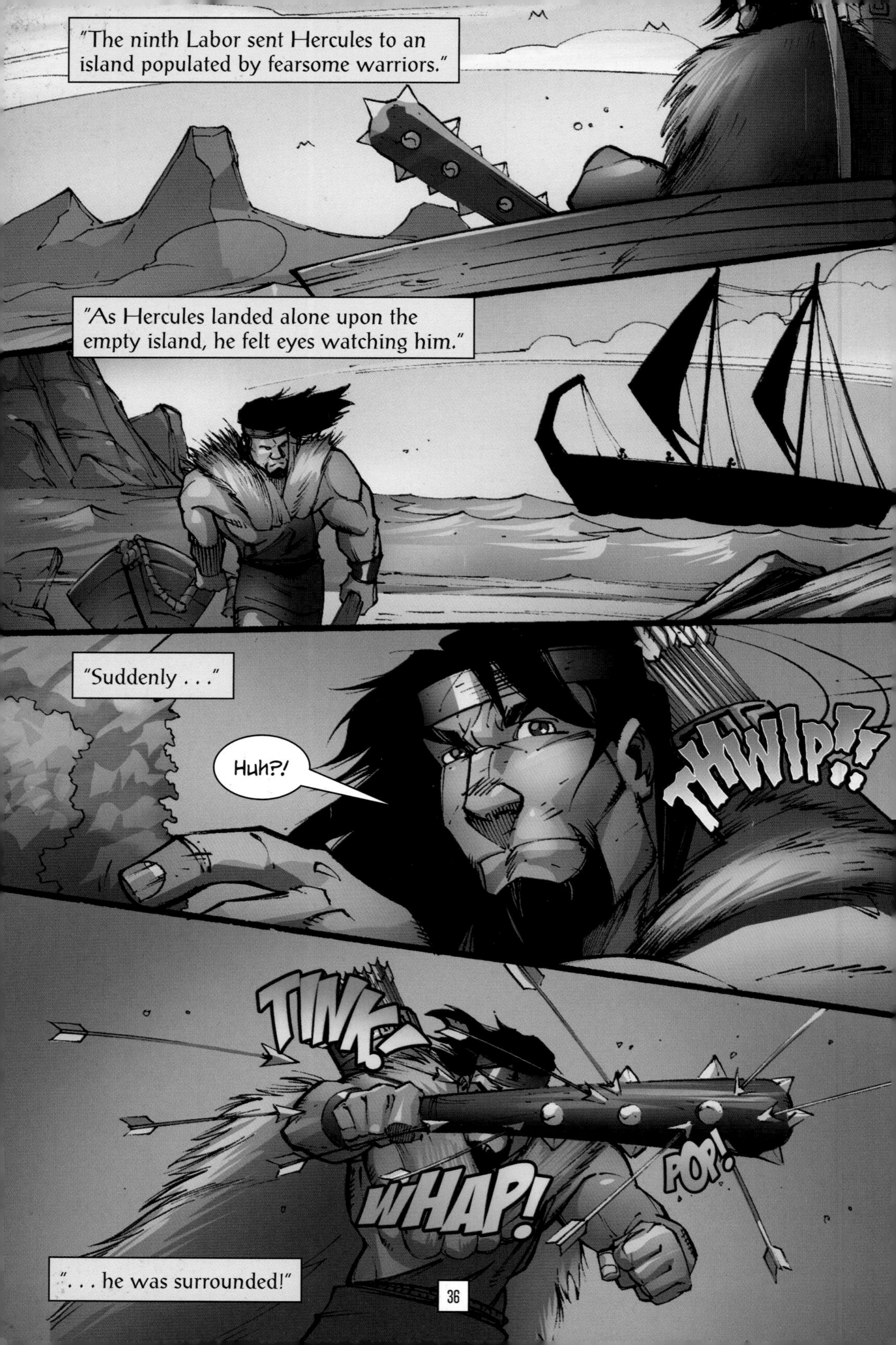
"The ninth Labor sent Hercules to an island populated by fearsome warriors."
"As Hercules landed alone upon the empty island, he felt eyes watching him."
"Suddenly . . ."
Huh?!
THWIP!!
TINK!
WHAP!
POP!
". . . he was surrounded!"

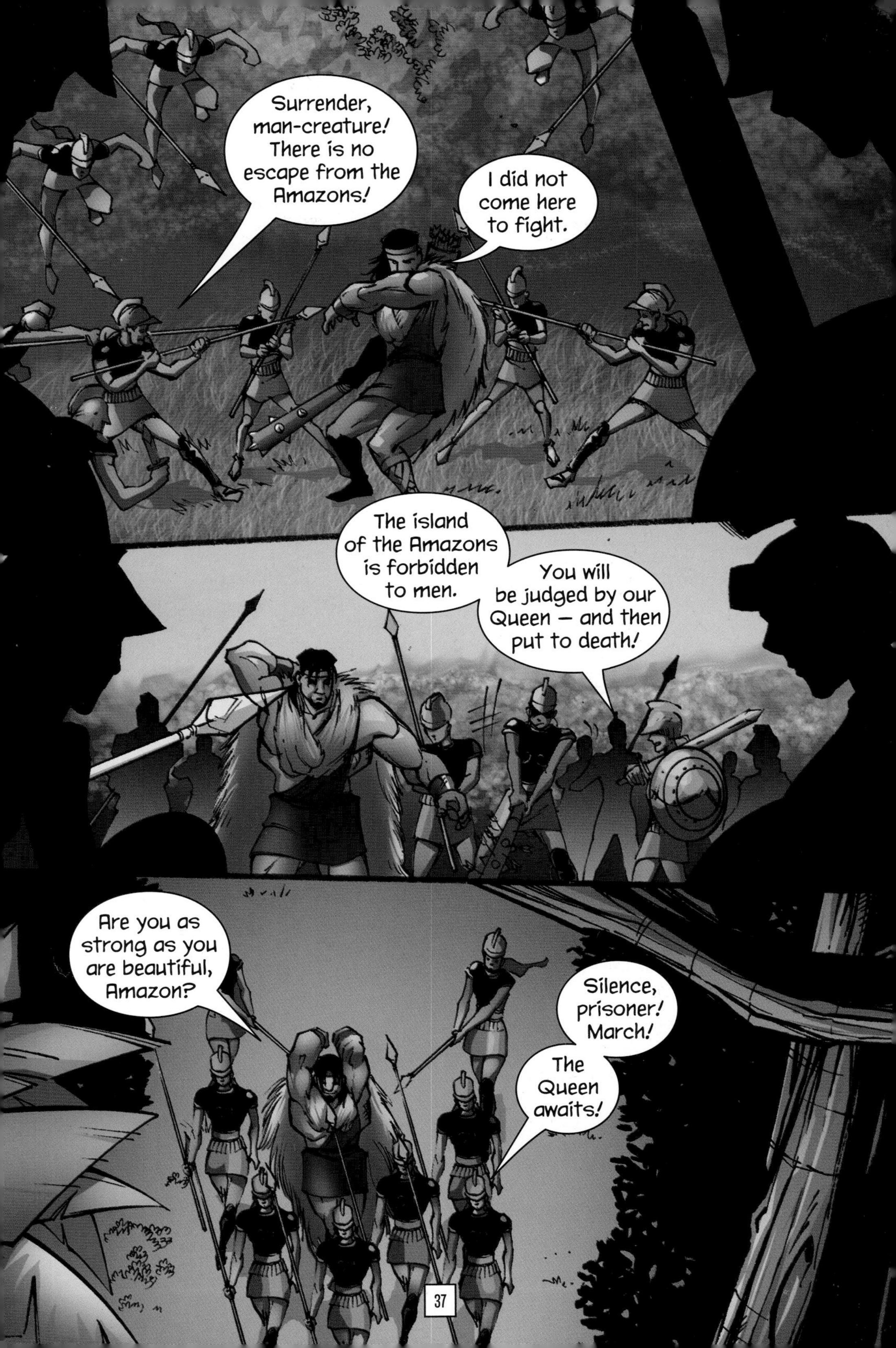
Surrender, man-creature! There is no escape from the Amazons!
I did not come here to fight.
The island of the Amazons is forbidden to men.
You will be judged by our Queen — and then put to death!
Are you as strong as you are beautiful, Amazon?
Silence, prisoner! March!
The Queen awaits!

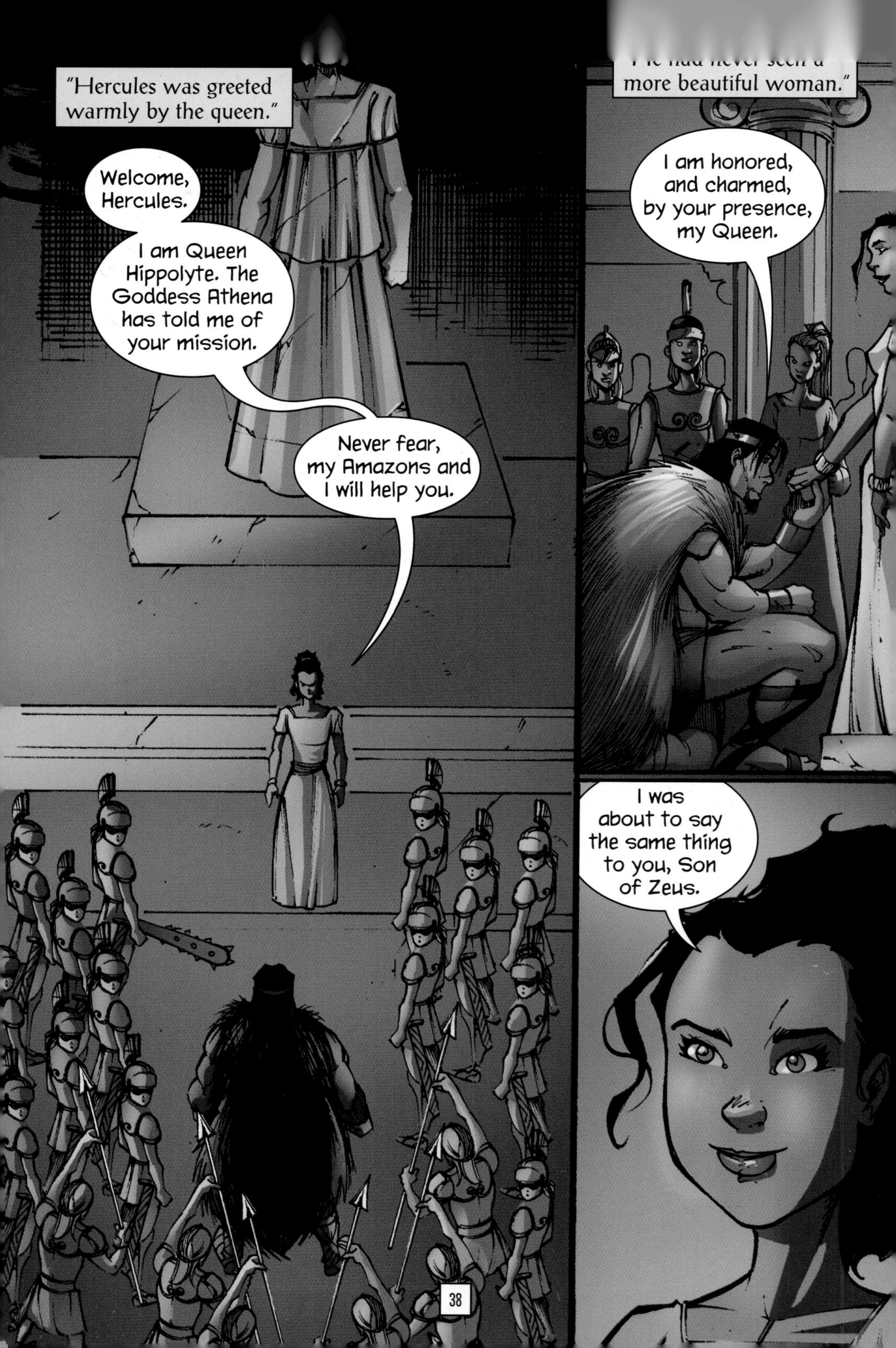
"Hercules was greeted warmly by the queen."
Welcome, Hercules.
I am Queen Hippolyte. The Goddess Athena has told me of your mission.
Never fear, my Amazons and I will help you.
more beautiful woman."
I am honored, and charmed, by your presence, my Queen.
I was about to say the same thing to you, Son of Zeus.

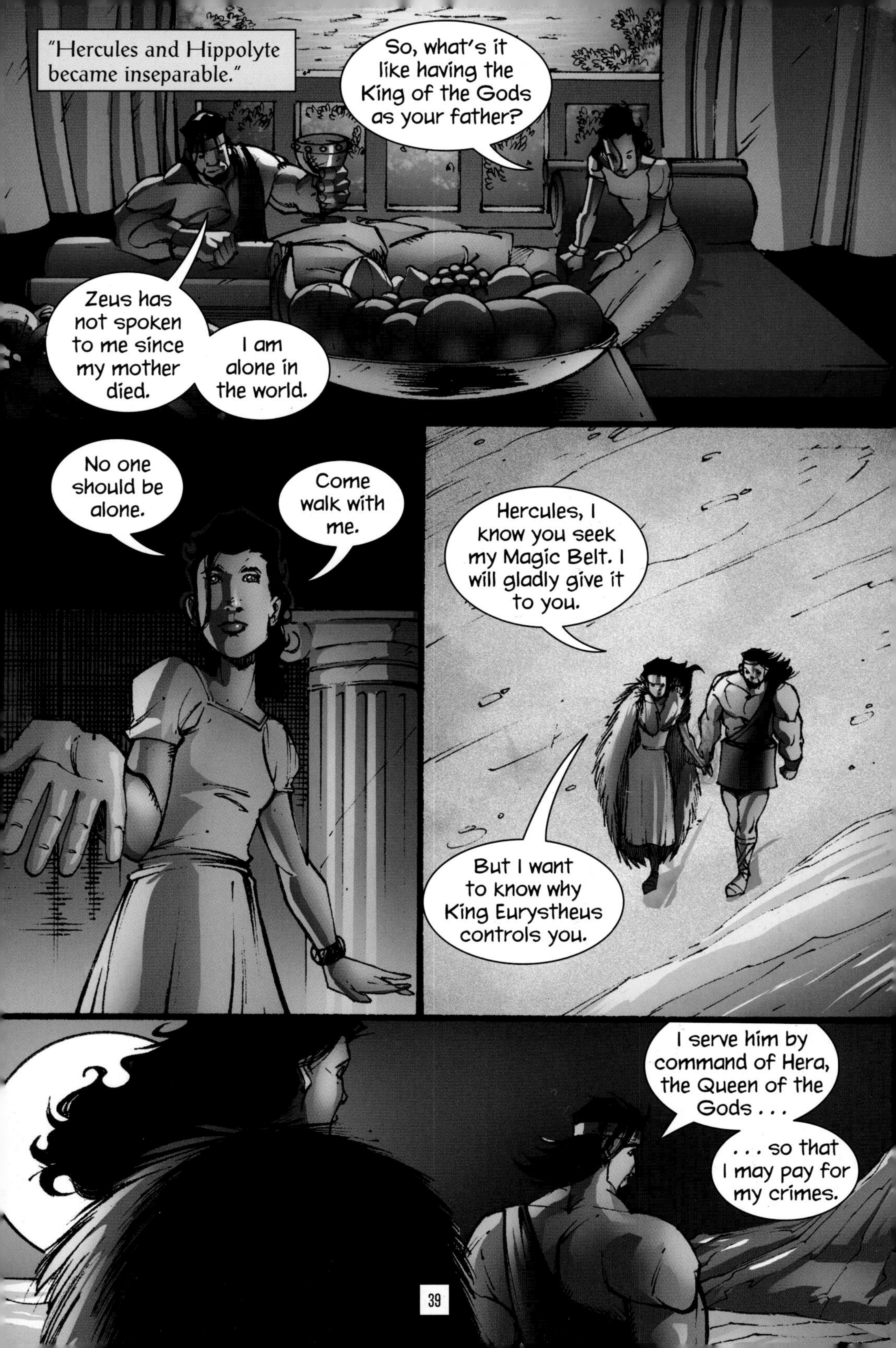
"Hercules and Hippolyte became inseparable."
So, what's it like having the King of the Gods as your father?
Zeus has not spoken to me since my mother died.
I am alone in the world.
No one should be alone.
Come walk with me.
Hercules, I know you seek my Magic Belt. I will gladly give it to you.
But I want to know why King Eurystheus controls you.
I serve him by command of Hera, the Queen of the Gods . . .
. . . so that I may pay for my crimes.

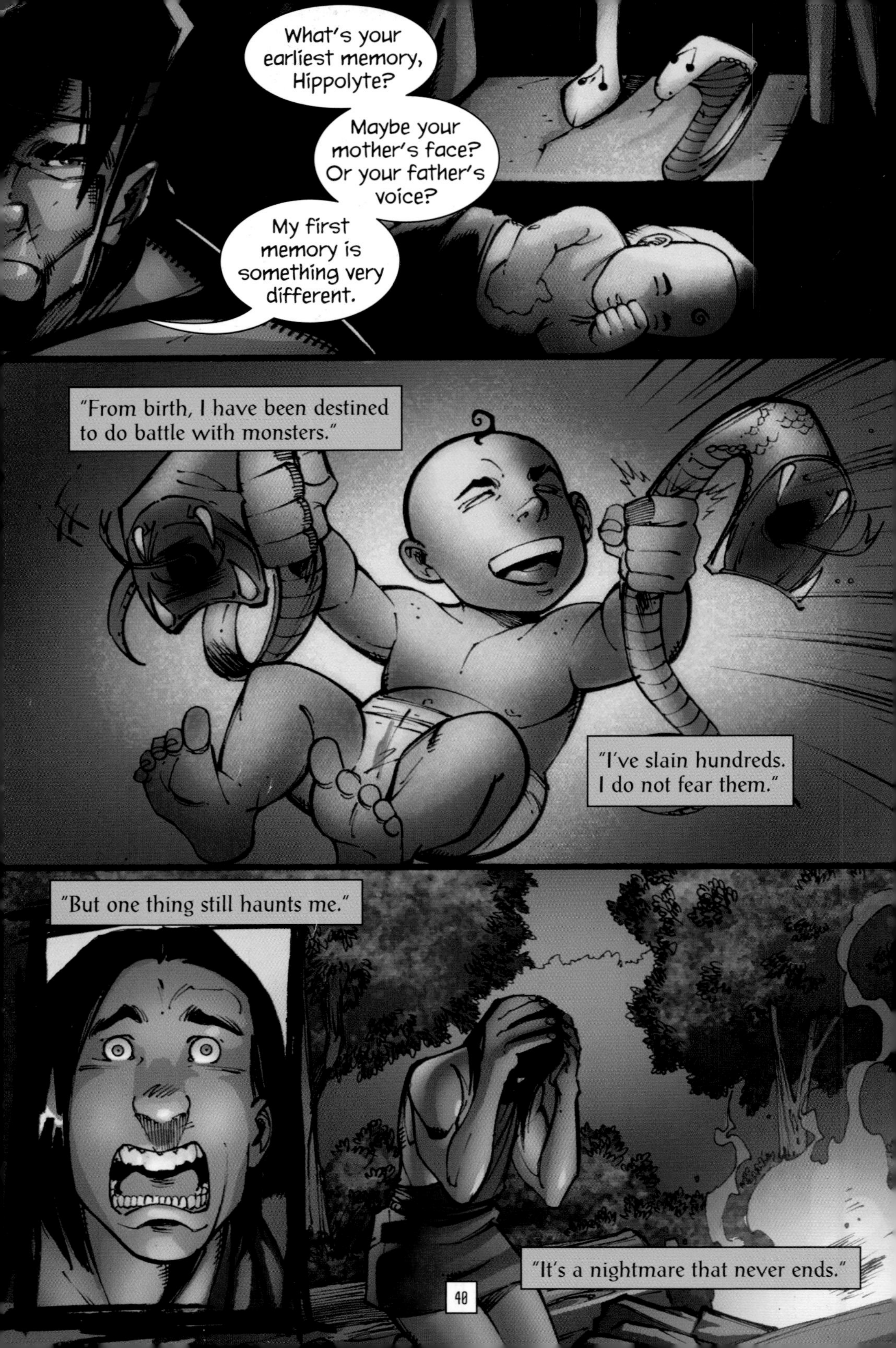

What's your earliest memory, Hippolyte?
Maybe your mother's face? Or your father's voice?
My first memory is something very different.
"From birth, I have been destined to do battle with monsters."
"I've slain hundreds. I do not fear them."
"But one thing still haunts me."
"It's a nightmare that never ends."

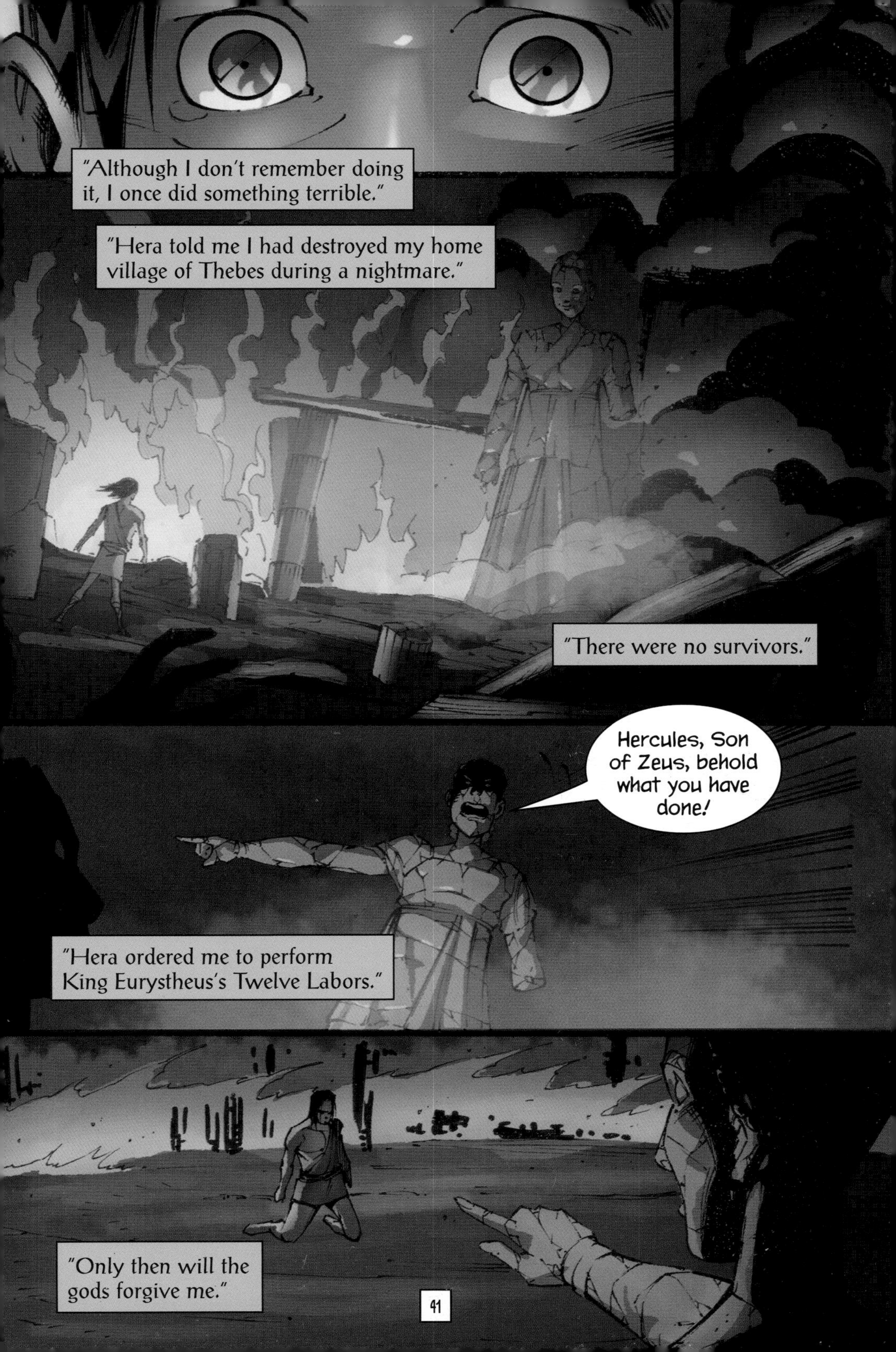
"Although I don't remember doing it, I once did something terrible."
"Hera told me I had destroyed my home village of Thebes during a nightmare."
"There were no survivors."
Hercules, Son of Zeus, behold what you have done!
"Hera ordered me to perform King Eurystheus's Twelve Labors."
"Only then will the gods forgive me."

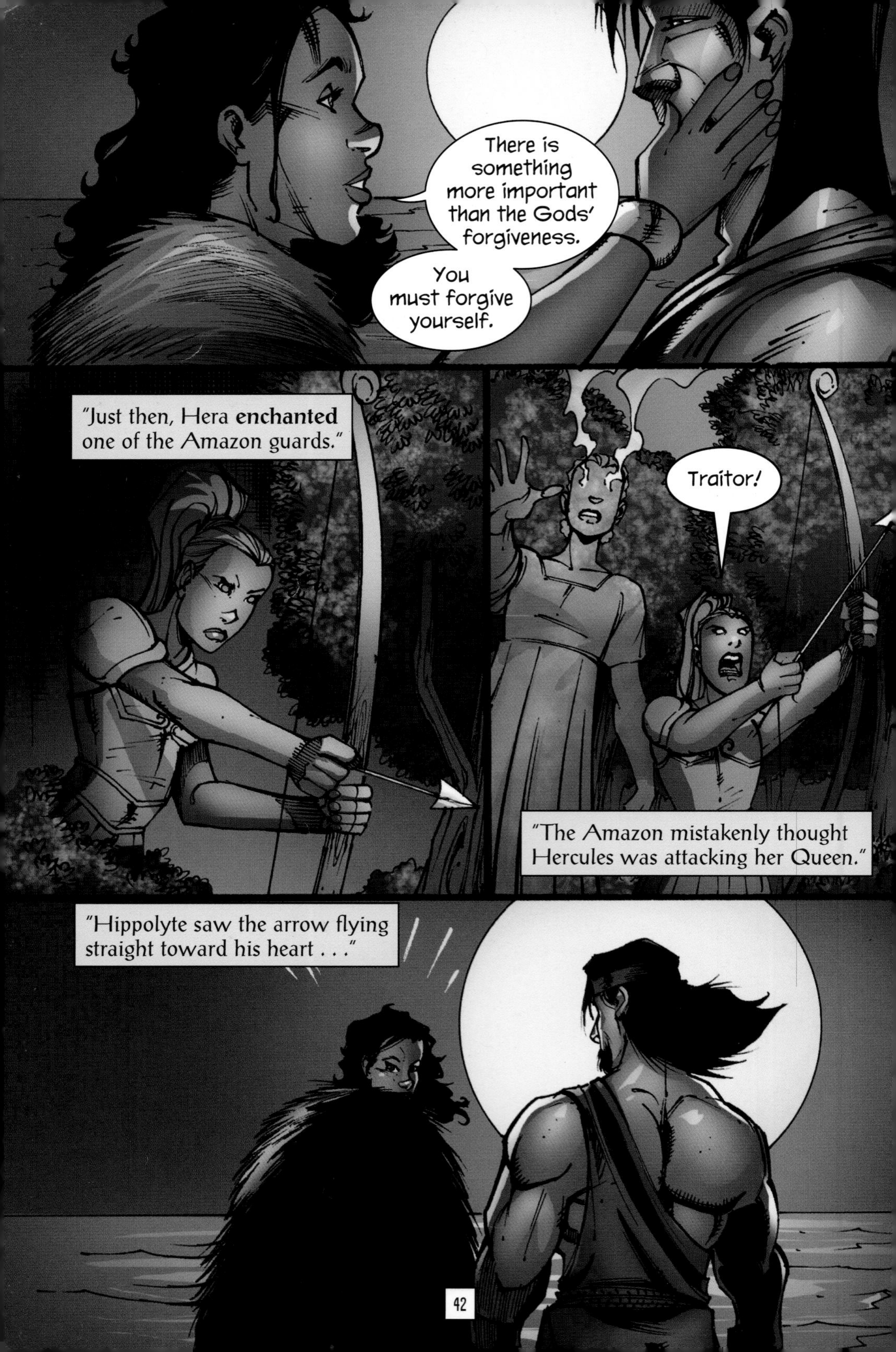
There is something more important than the Gods' forgiveness.
You must forgive yourself.
"Just then, Hera **enchanted** one of the Amazon guards."
Traitor!
"The Amazon mistakenly thought Hercules was attacking her Queen."
"Hippolyte saw the arrow flying straight toward his heart . . ."

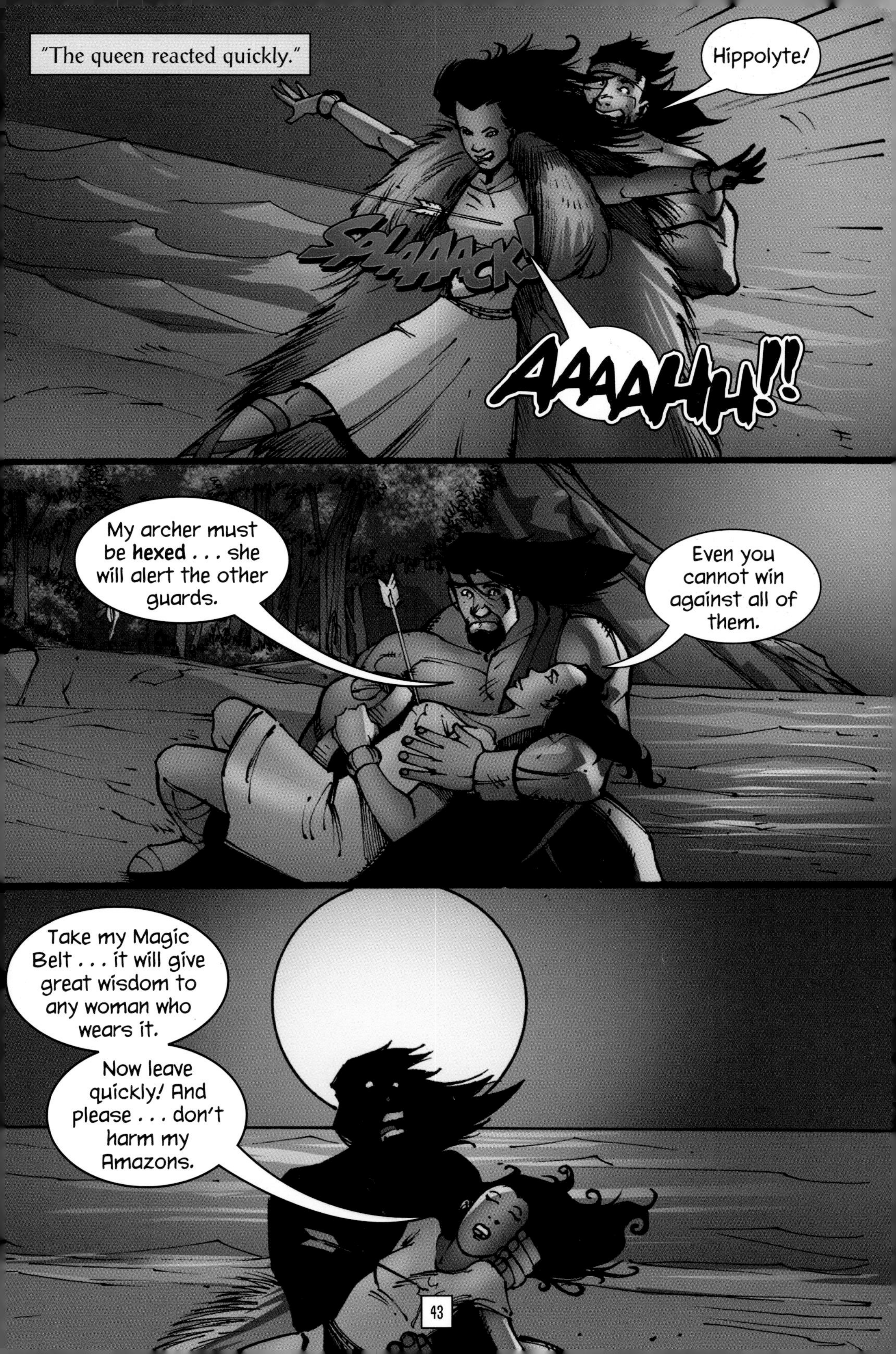
"The queen reacted quickly."
Hippolyte!
SPLAAACK!
AAAAHH!!
My archer must be hexed . . . she will alert the other guards.
Even you cannot win against all of them.
Take my Magic Belt . . . it will give great wisdom to any woman who wears it.
Now leave quickly! And please . . . don't harm my Amazons.

# CHAPTER 4

# A MIGHTY BURDEN

"With a heavy heart, Hercules obeyed Queen Hippolyte and fled."

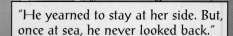

"He yearned to stay at her side. But, once at sea, he never looked back."

THWAP!!

WHAP!

THUD

"Instead, he gazed at the gift she had given him as he remembered her great beauty and wisdom."

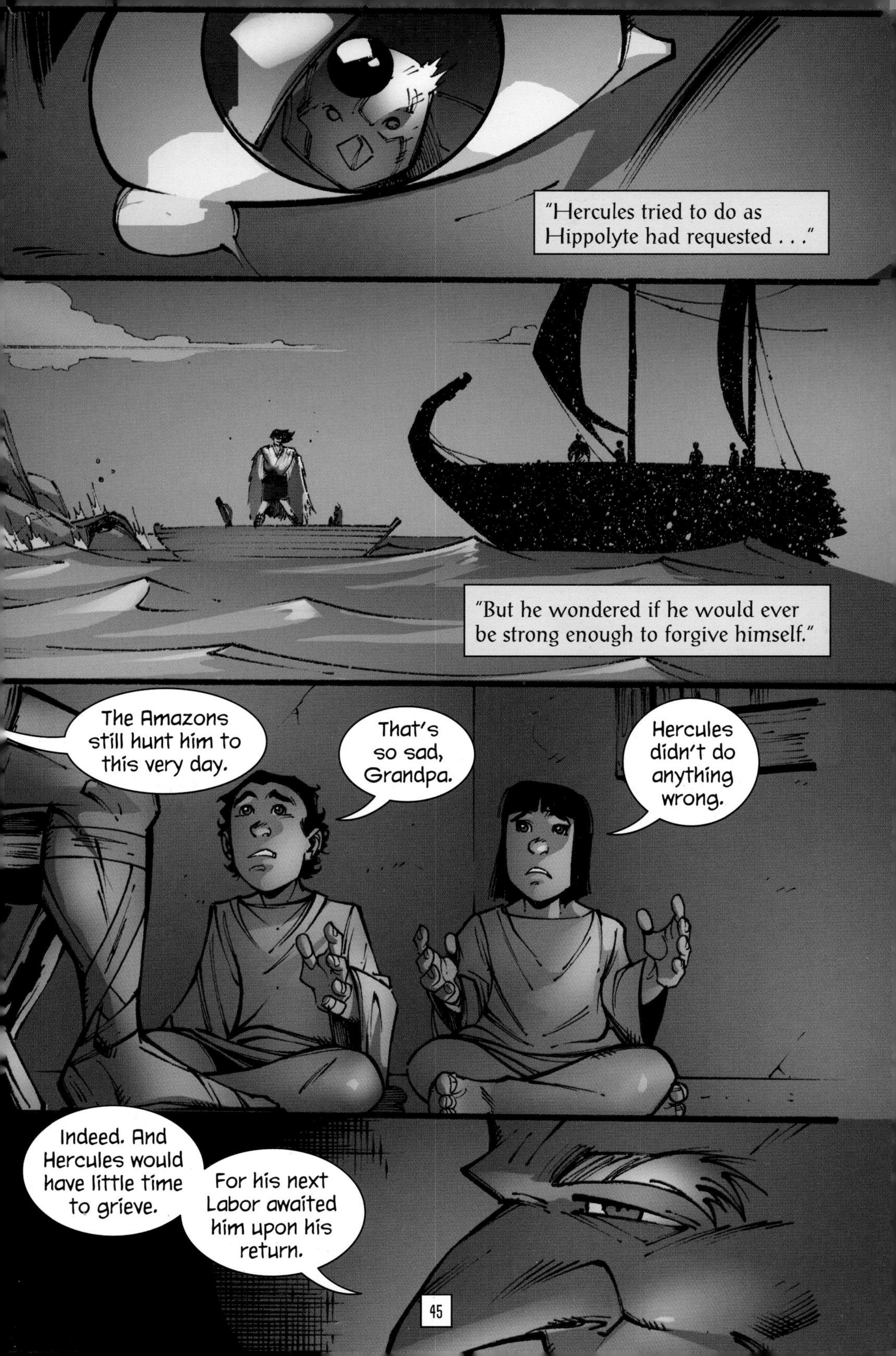
"Hercules tried to do as Hippolyte had requested . . ."
"But he wondered if he would ever be strong enough to forgive himself."
The Amazons still hunt him to this very day.
That's so sad, Grandpa.
Hercules didn't do anything wrong.
Indeed. And Hercules would have little time to grieve.
For his next Labor awaited him upon his return.

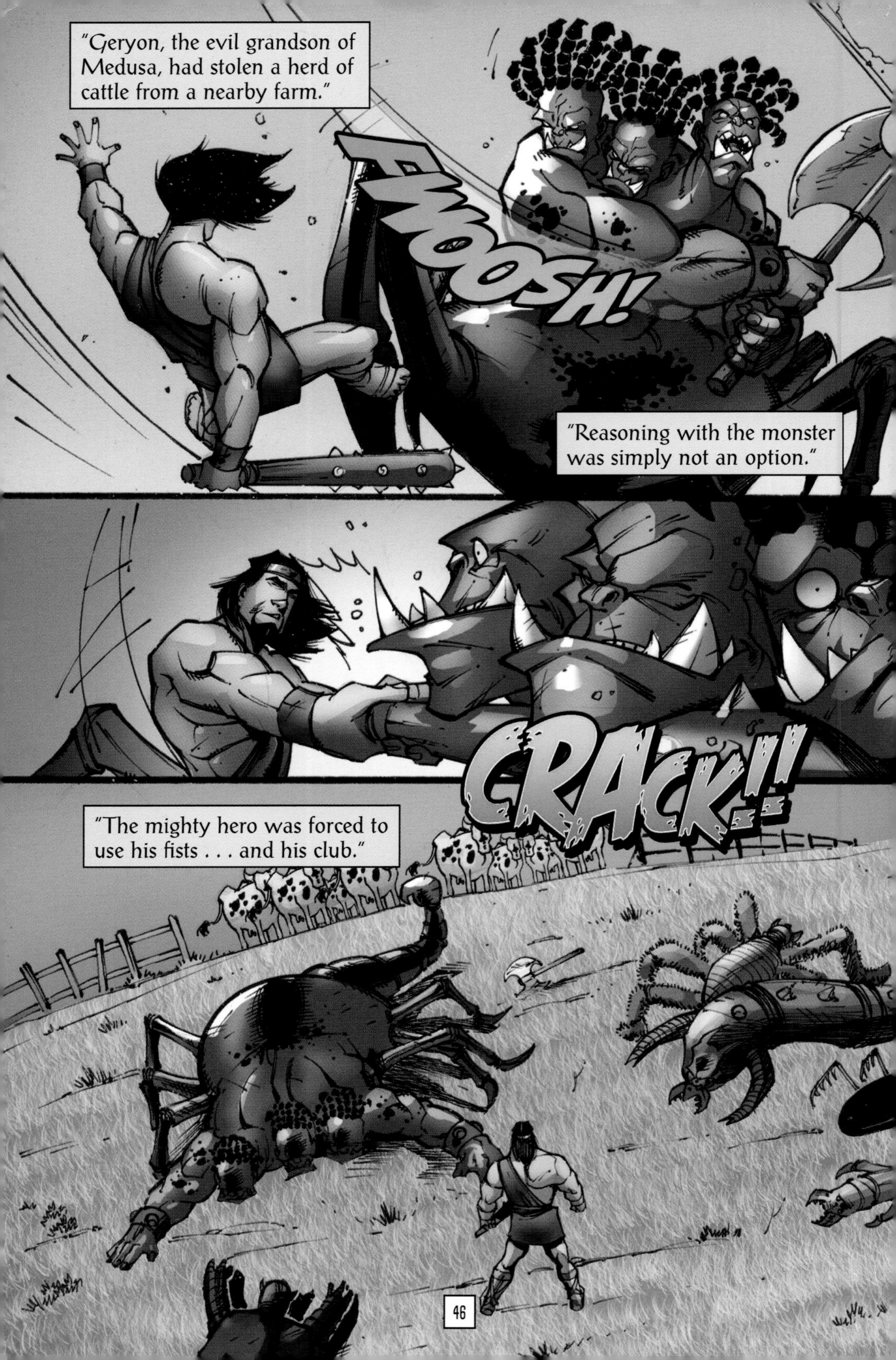
"Geryon, the evil grandson of Medusa, had stolen a herd of cattle from a nearby farm."
FWOOSH!
"Reasoning with the monster was simply not an option."
CRACK!!
"The mighty hero was forced to use his fists . . . and his club."

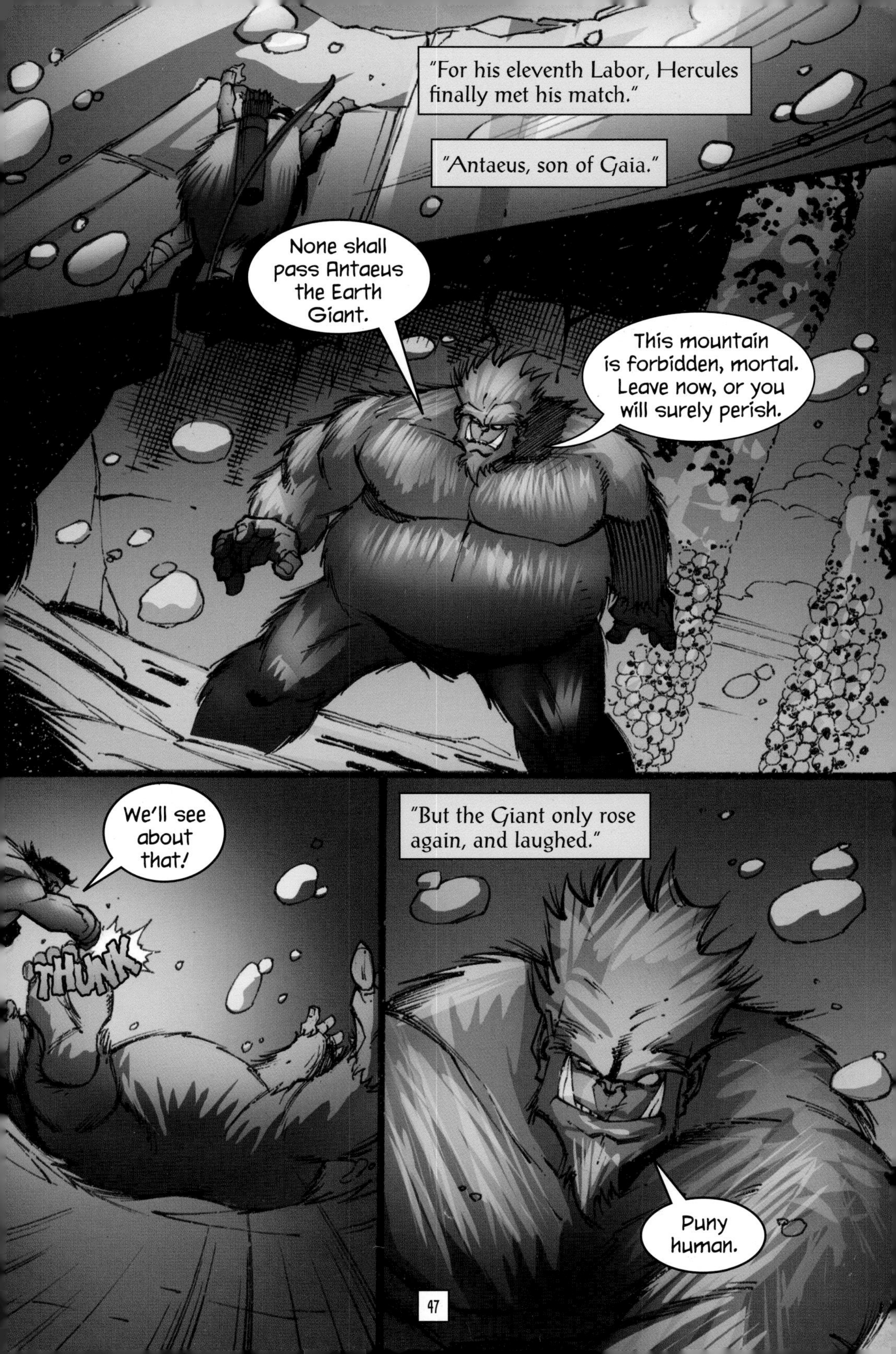
"For his eleventh Labor, Hercules finally met his match."
"Antaeus, son of Gaia."
None shall pass Antaeus the Earth Giant.
This mountain is forbidden, mortal. Leave now, or you will surely perish.
We'll see about that!
THUNK
"But the Giant only rose again, and laughed."
Puny human.

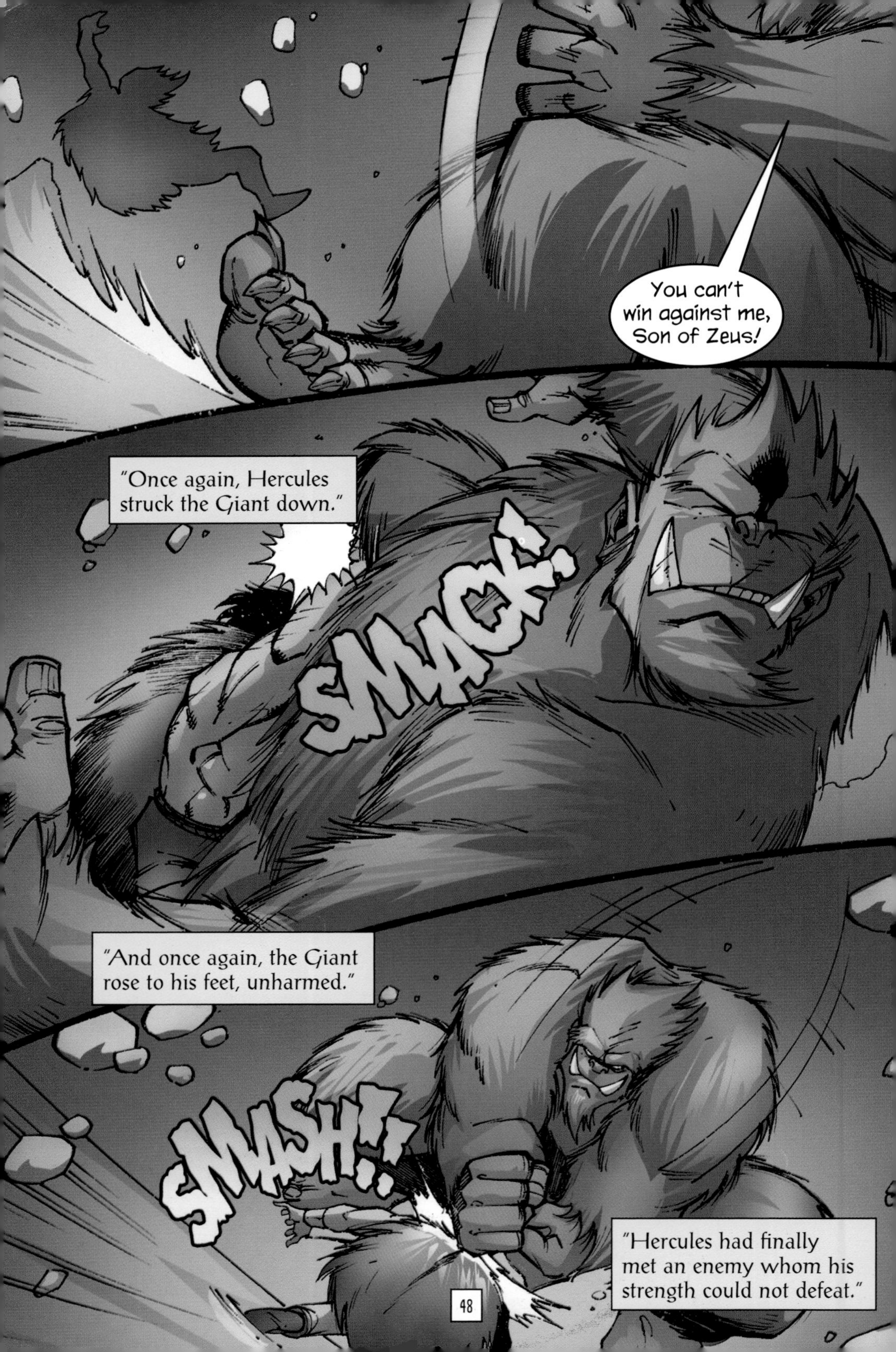
You can't win against me, Son of Zeus!
"Once again, Hercules struck the Giant down."
SMACK!
"And once again, the Giant rose to his feet, unharmed."
SMASH!!
"Hercules had finally met an enemy whom his strength could not defeat."

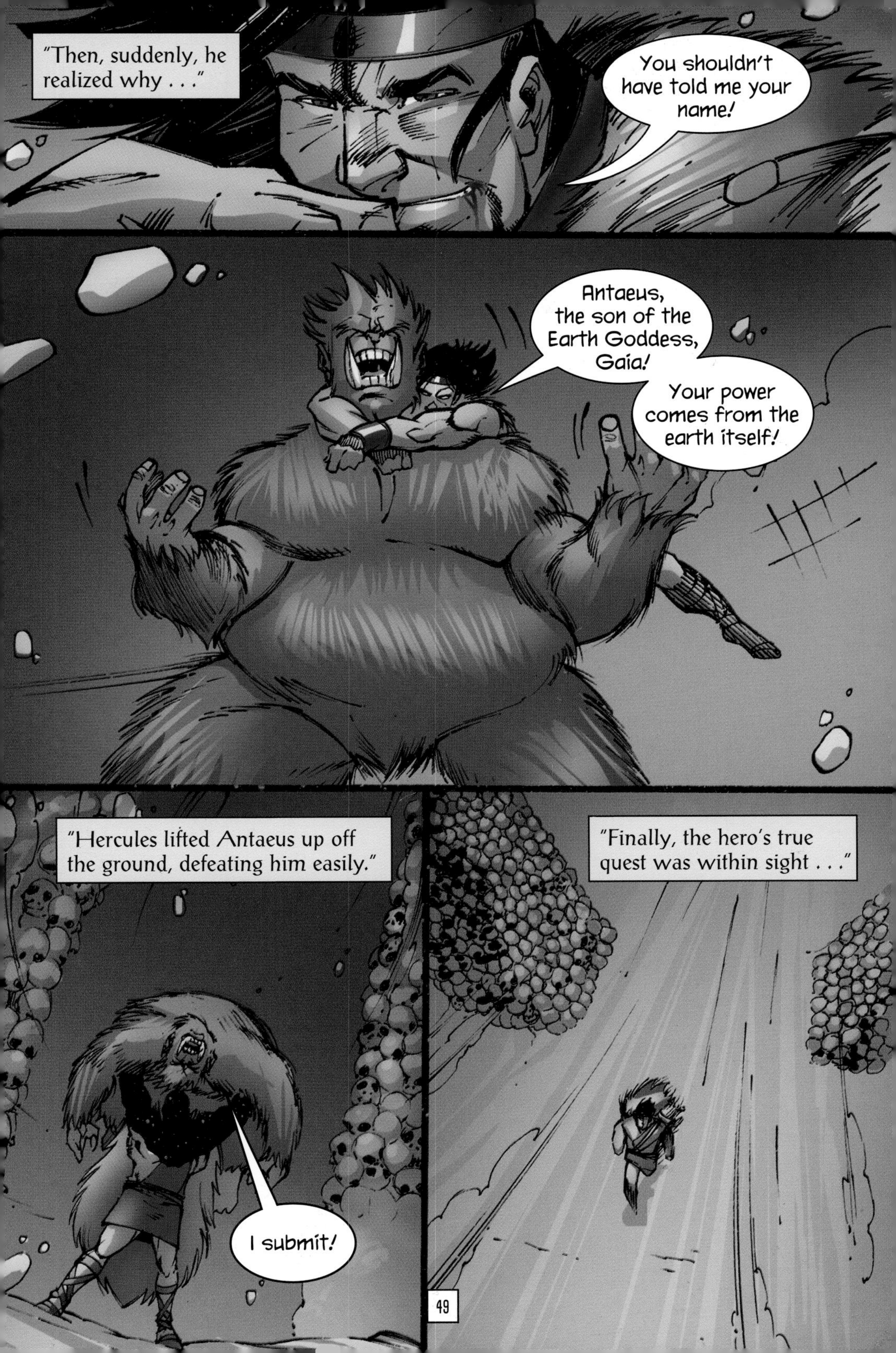
"Then, suddenly, he realized why . . ."
You shouldn't have told me your name!
Antaeus, the son of the Earth Goddess, Gaia!
Your power comes from the earth itself!
"Hercules lifted Antaeus up off the ground, defeating him easily."
I submit!
"Finally, the hero's true quest was within sight . . ."

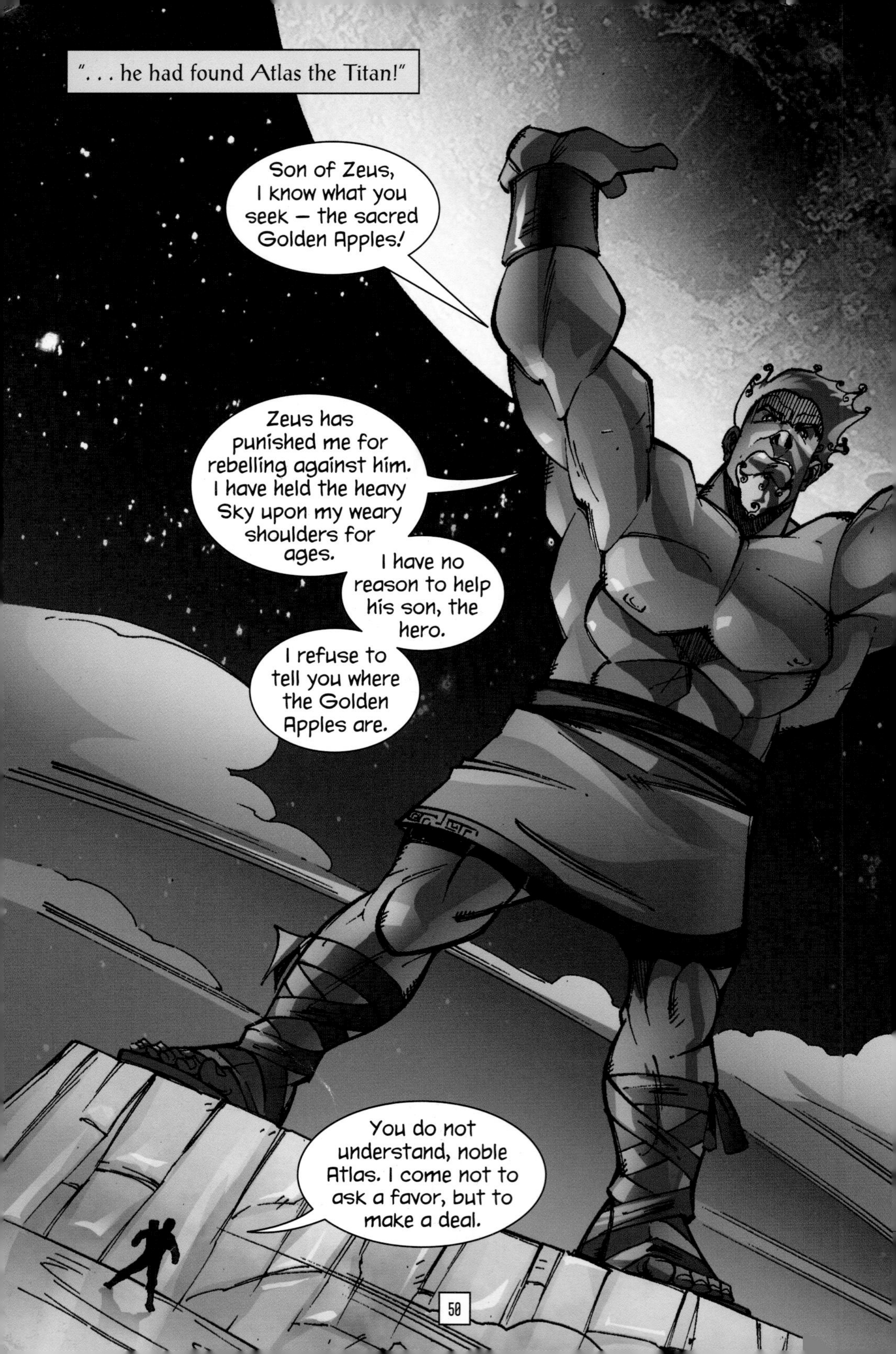
". . . he had found Atlas the Titan!"
Son of Zeus, I know what you seek — the sacred Golden Apples!
Zeus has punished me for rebelling against him. I have held the heavy Sky upon my weary shoulders for ages.
I have no reason to help his son, the hero.
I refuse to tell you where the Golden Apples are.
You do not understand, noble Atlas. I come not to ask a favor, but to make a deal.

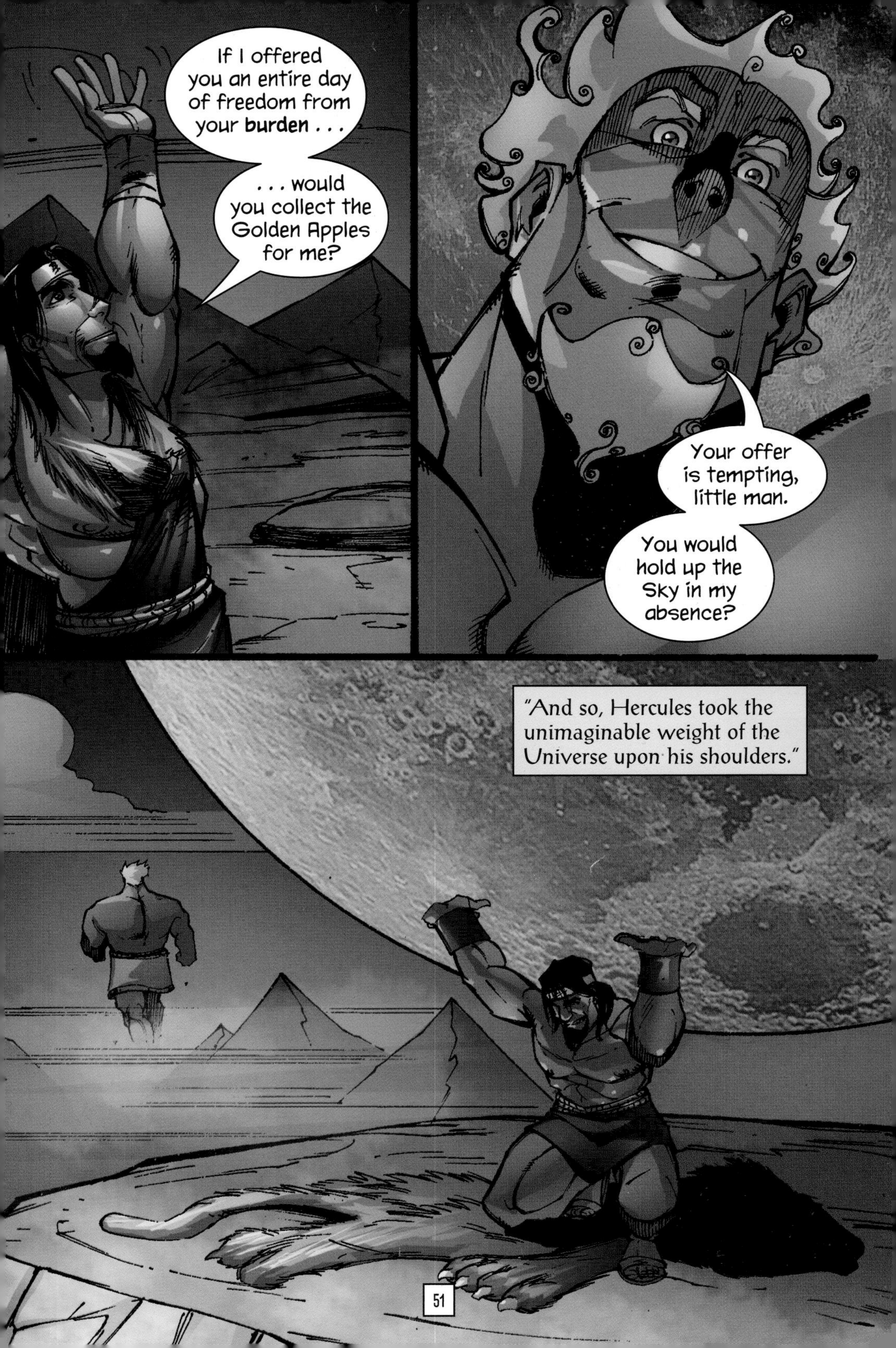
If I offered you an entire day of freedom from your **burden** . . .
. . . would you collect the Golden Apples for me?
Your offer is tempting, little man.
You would hold up the Sky in my absence?
"And so, Hercules took the unimaginable weight of the Universe upon his shoulders."

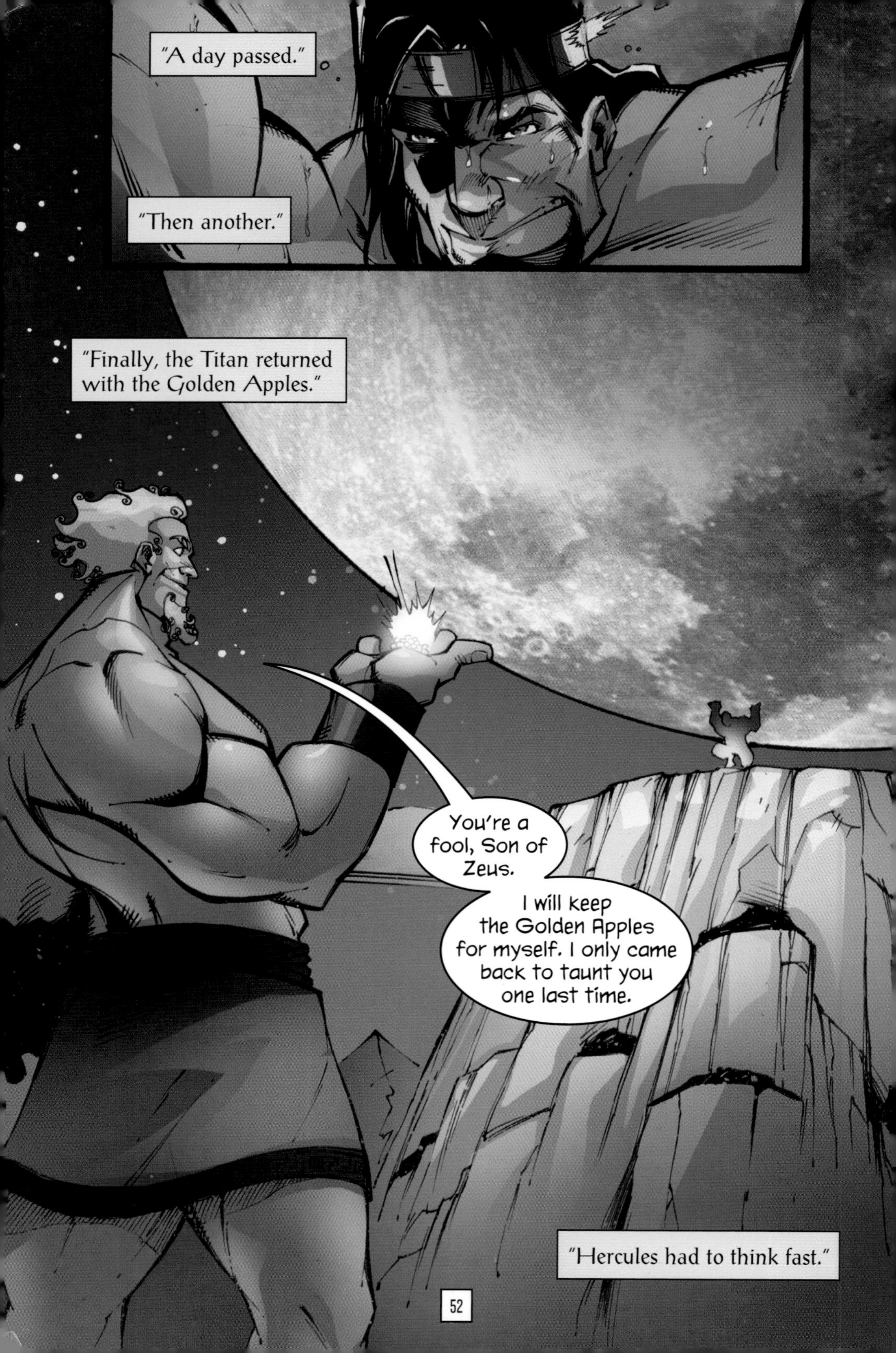
"A day passed."
"Then another."
"Finally, the Titan returned with the Golden Apples."
You're a fool, Son of Zeus.
I will keep the Golden Apples for myself. I only came back to taunt you one last time.
"Hercules had to think fast."

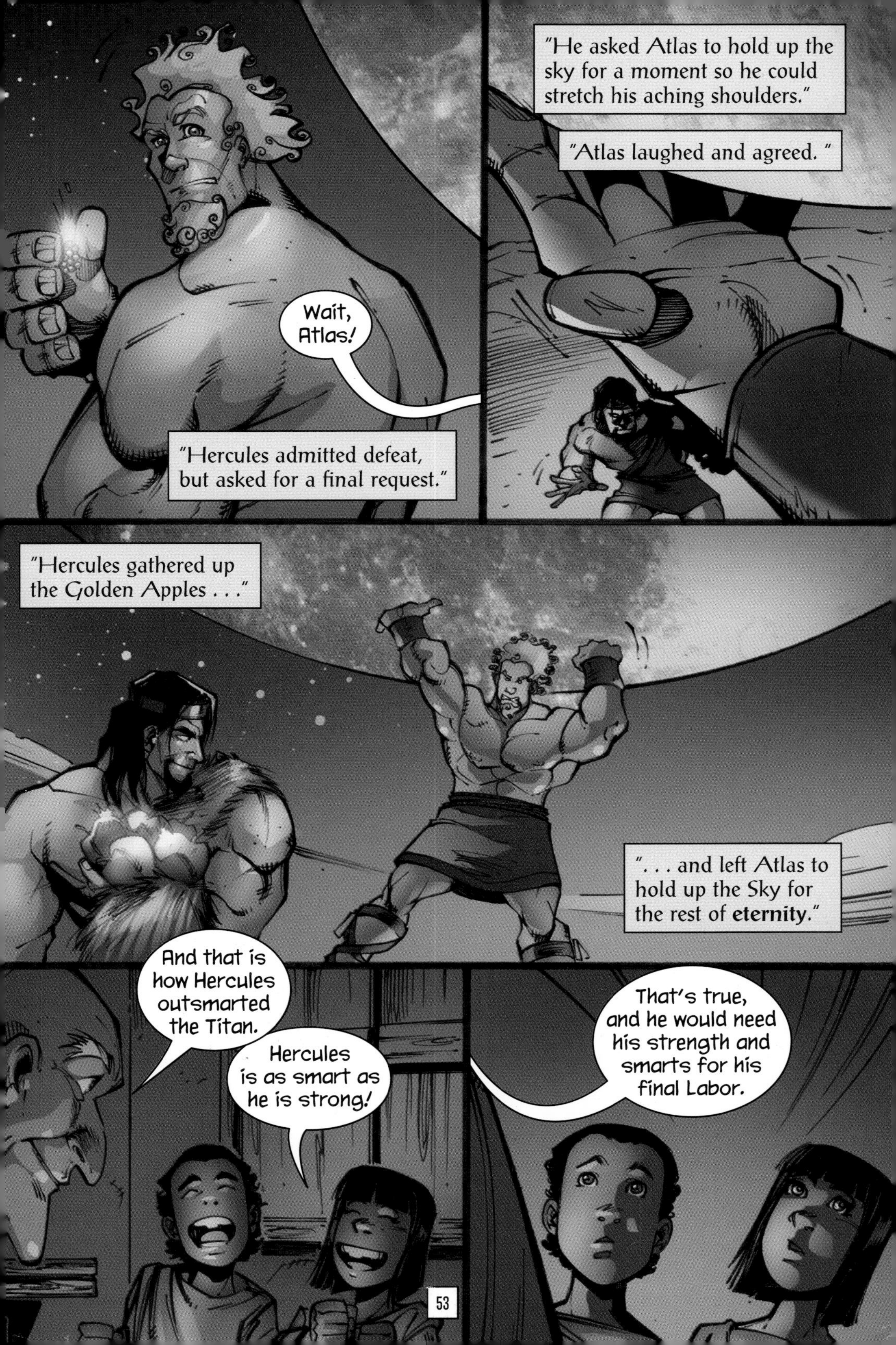
"Hercules admitted defeat, but asked for a final request."
Wait, Atlas!
"He asked Atlas to hold up the sky for a moment so he could stretch his aching shoulders."
"Atlas laughed and agreed. "
"Hercules gathered up the Golden Apples . . ."
". . . and left Atlas to hold up the Sky for the rest of **eternity**."
And that is how Hercules outsmarted the Titan.
Hercules is as smart as he is strong!
That's true, and he would need his strength and smarts for his final Labor.

# CHAPTER 5

# LEGENDS NEVER DIE

"The twelfth Labor took Hercules deep into the Land of the Dead."

"The hero bravely ventured into the haunted cave."

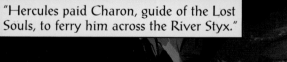

"Hercules paid Charon, guide of the Lost Souls, to ferry him across the River Styx."

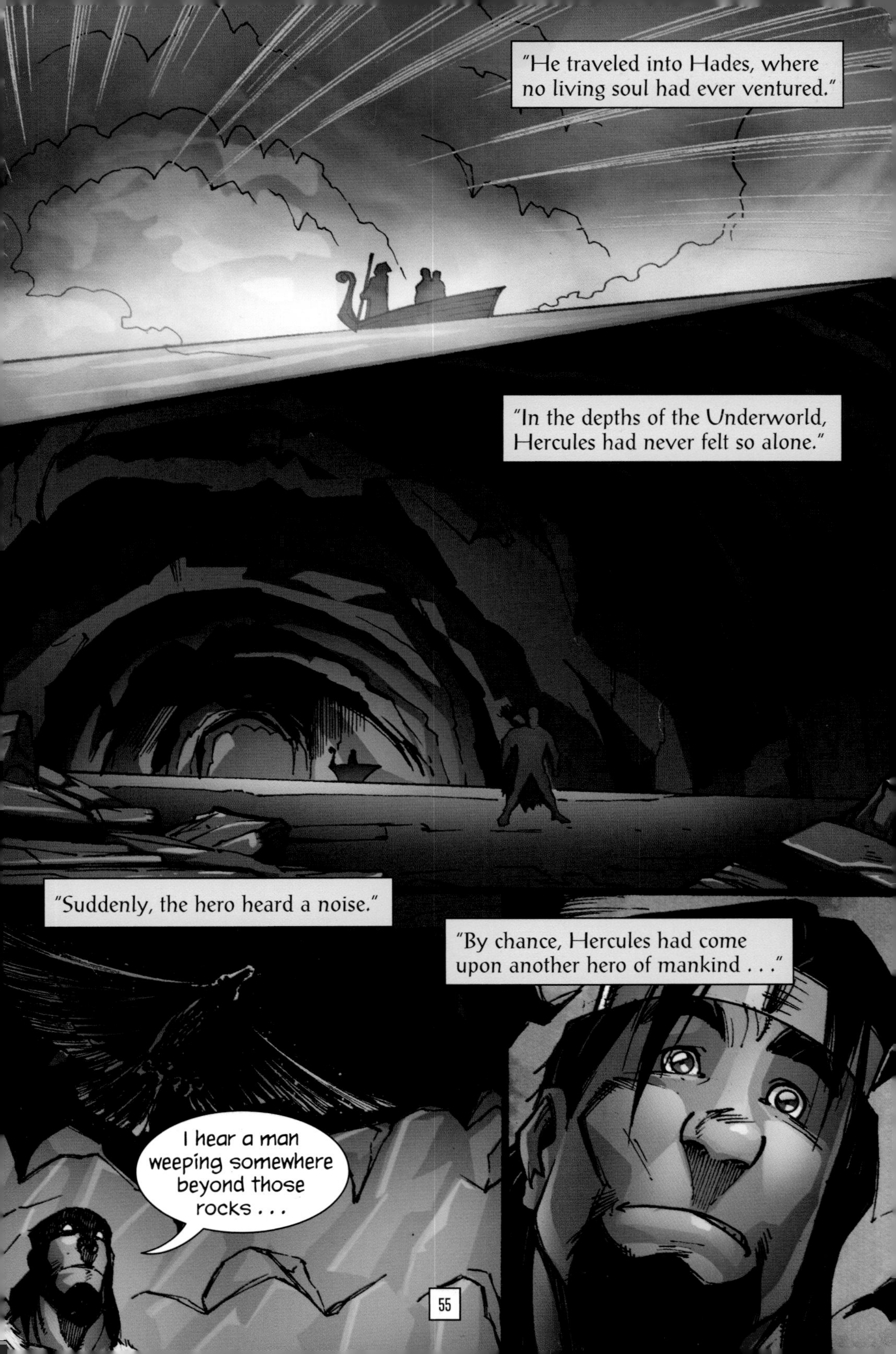
"He traveled into Hades, where no living soul had ever ventured."
"In the depths of the Underworld, Hercules had never felt so alone."
"Suddenly, the hero heard a noise."
I hear a man weeping somewhere beyond those rocks . . .
"By chance, Hercules had come upon another hero of mankind . . ."

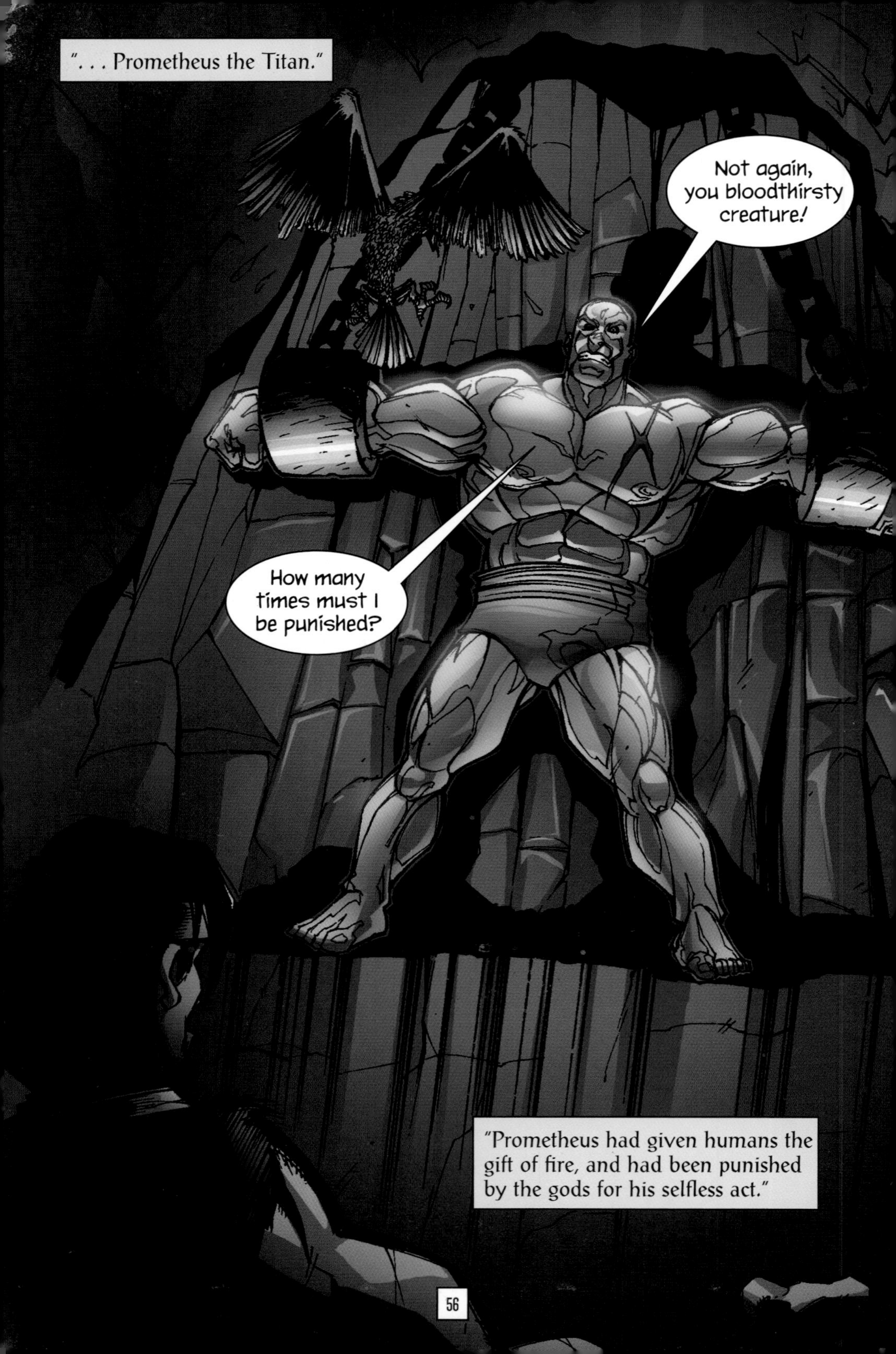
". . . Prometheus the Titan."
Not again, you bloodthirsty creature!
How many times must I be punished?
"Prometheus had given humans the gift of fire, and had been punished by the gods for his selfless act."

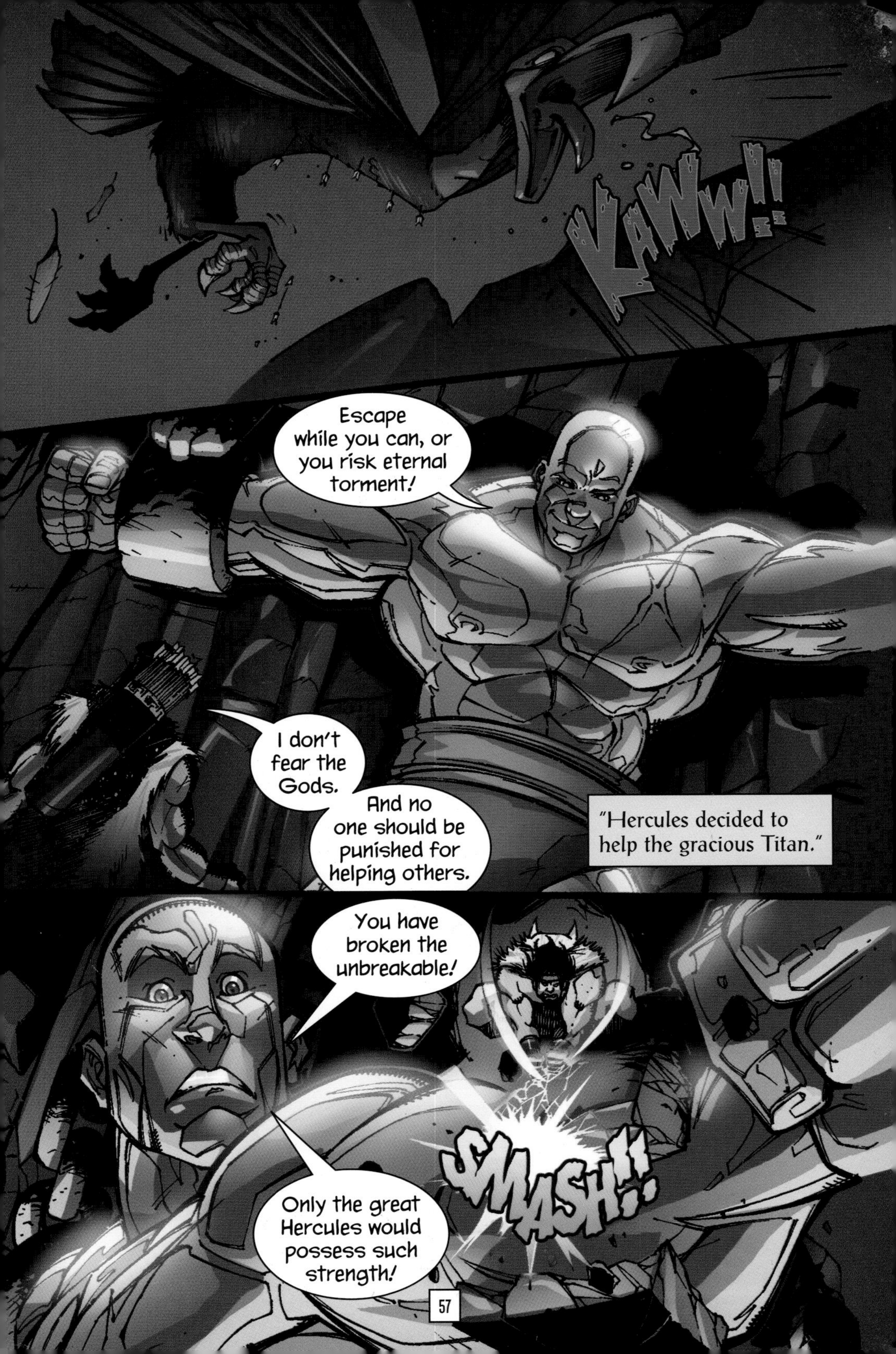
KAWW!!
Escape while you can, or you risk eternal torment!
I don't fear the Gods.
And no one should be punished for helping others.
"Hercules decided to help the gracious Titan."
You have broken the unbreakable!
SMASH!!
Only the great Hercules would possess such strength!

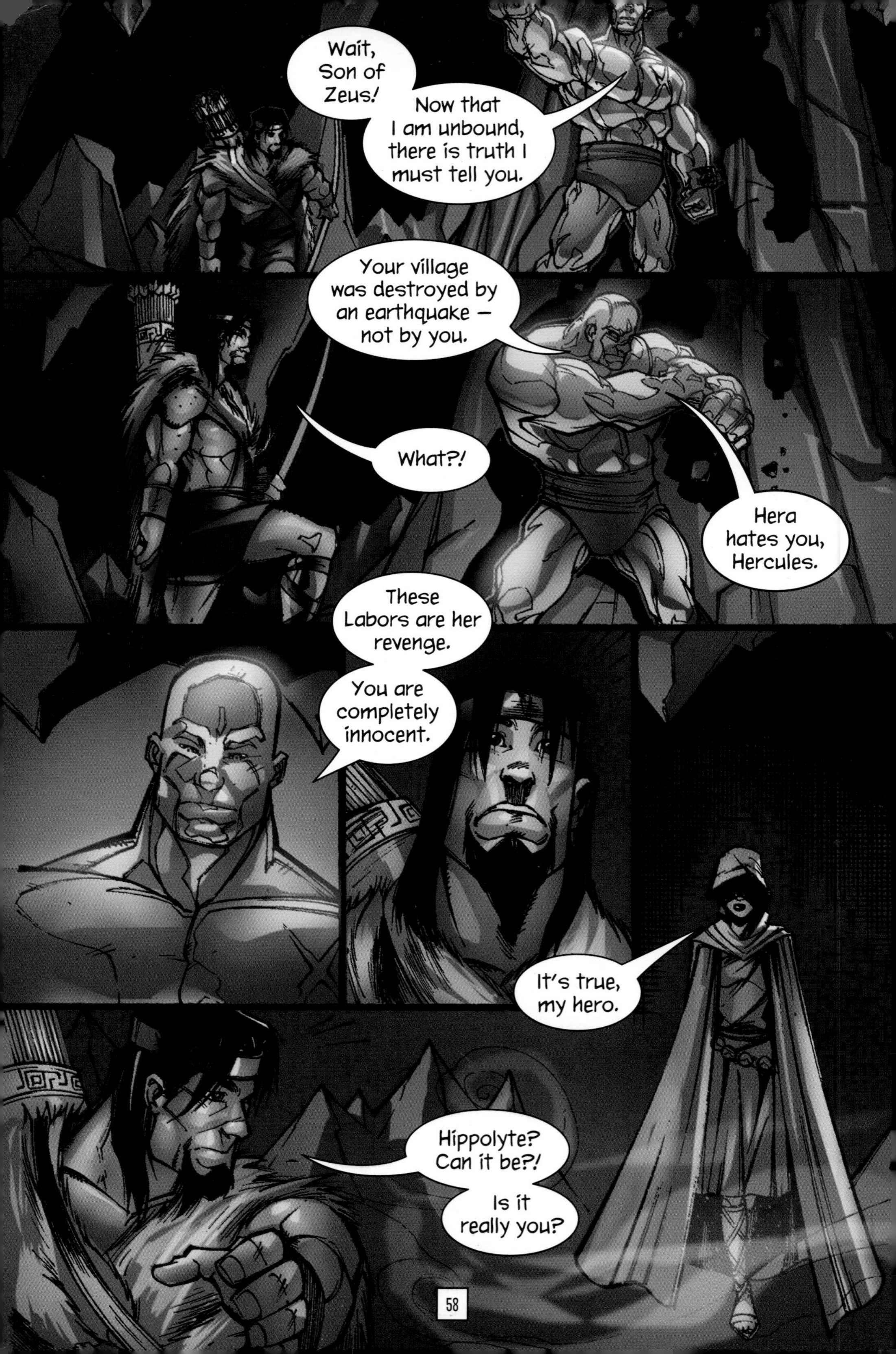
Wait, Son of Zeus!
Now that I am unbound, there is truth I must tell you.
Your village was destroyed by an earthquake — not by you.
What?!
Hera hates you, Hercules.
These Labors are her revenge.
You are completely innocent.
It's true, my hero.
Hippolyte? Can it be?!
Is it really you?

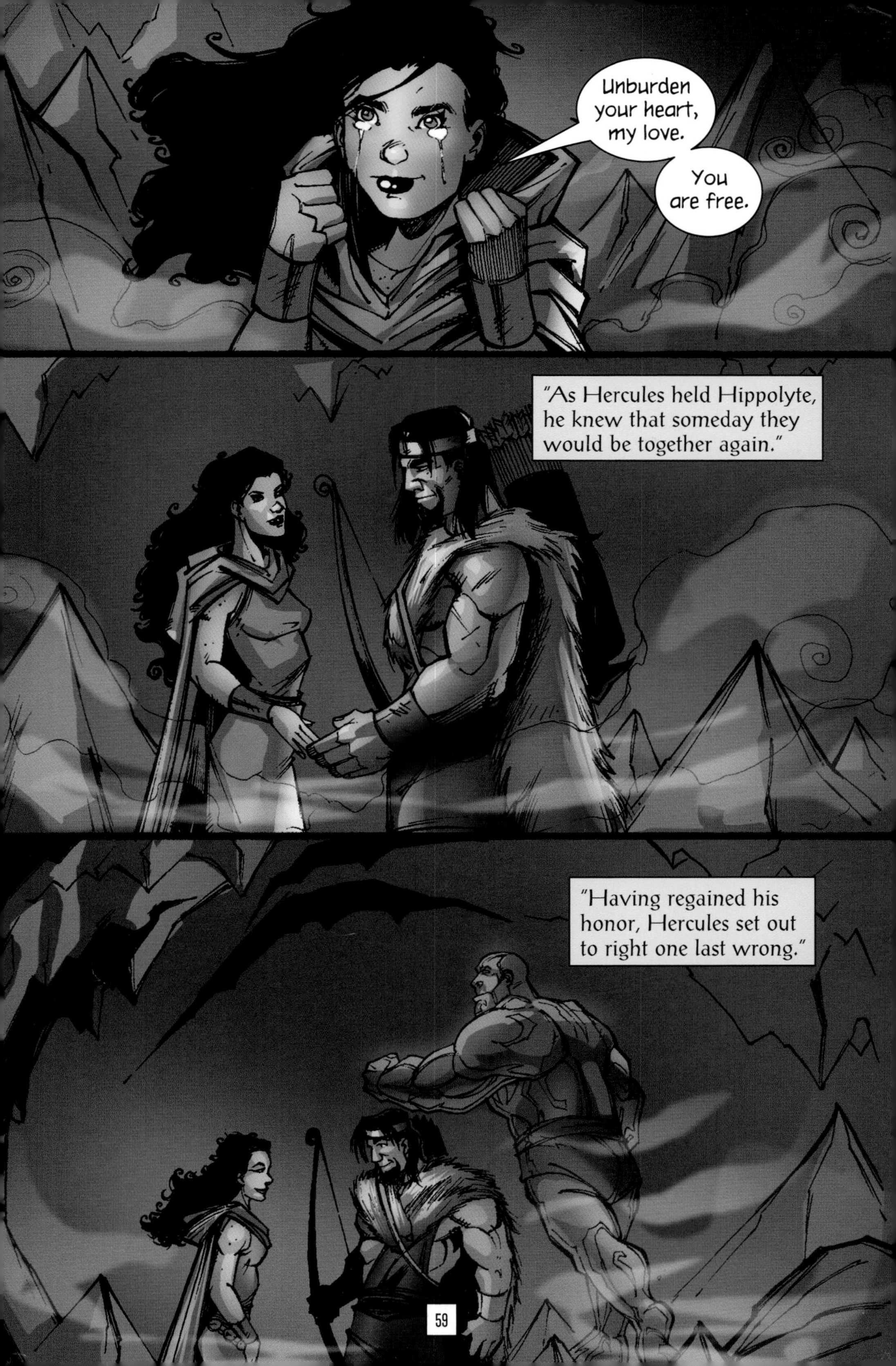
Unburden your heart, my love.
You are free.
"As Hercules held Hippolyte, he knew that someday they would be together again."
"Having regained his honor, Hercules set out to right one last wrong."

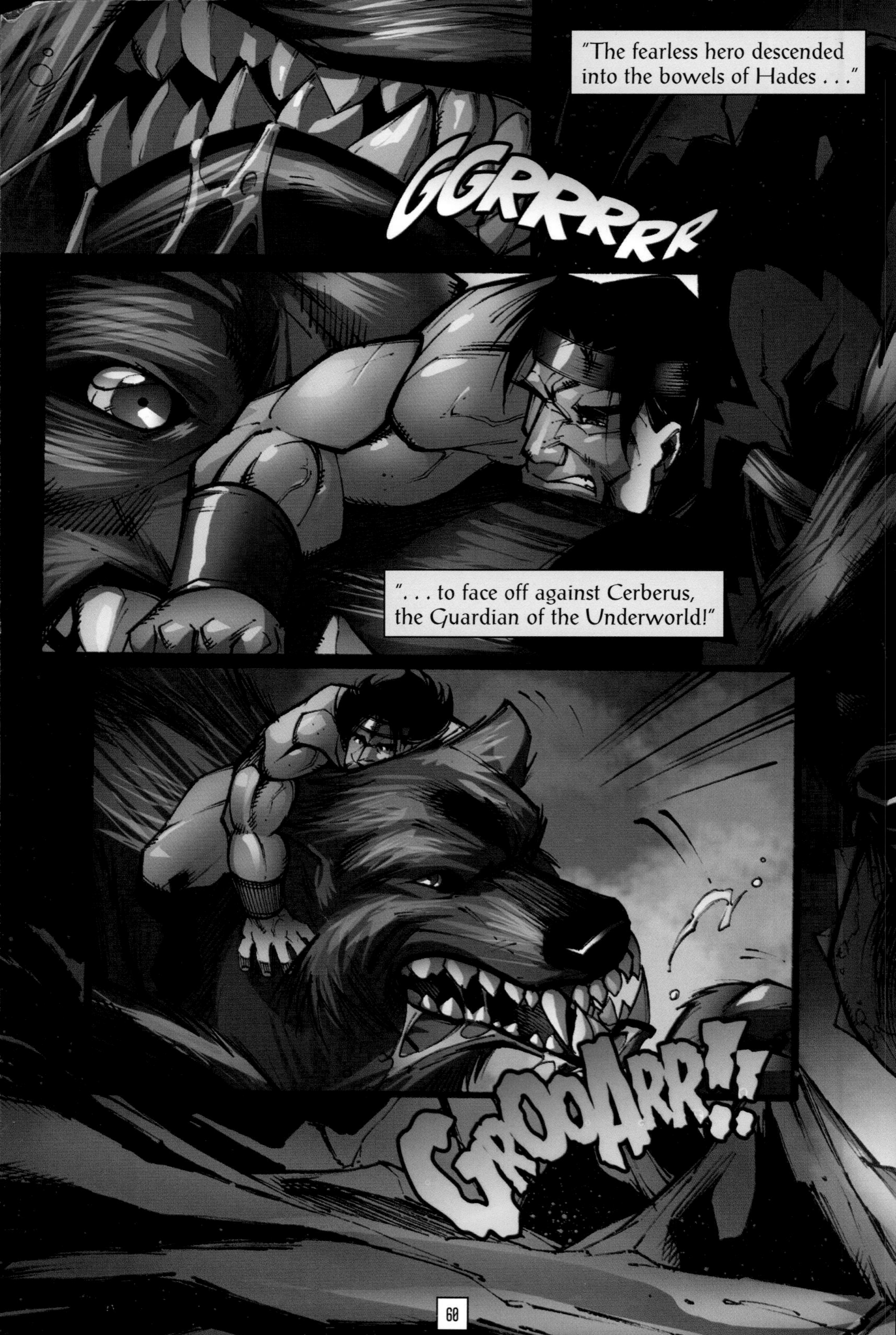

"The fearless hero descended into the bowels of Hades . . ."
GGRRRRR
". . . to face off against Cerberus, the Guardian of the Underworld!"
GROOARR!!

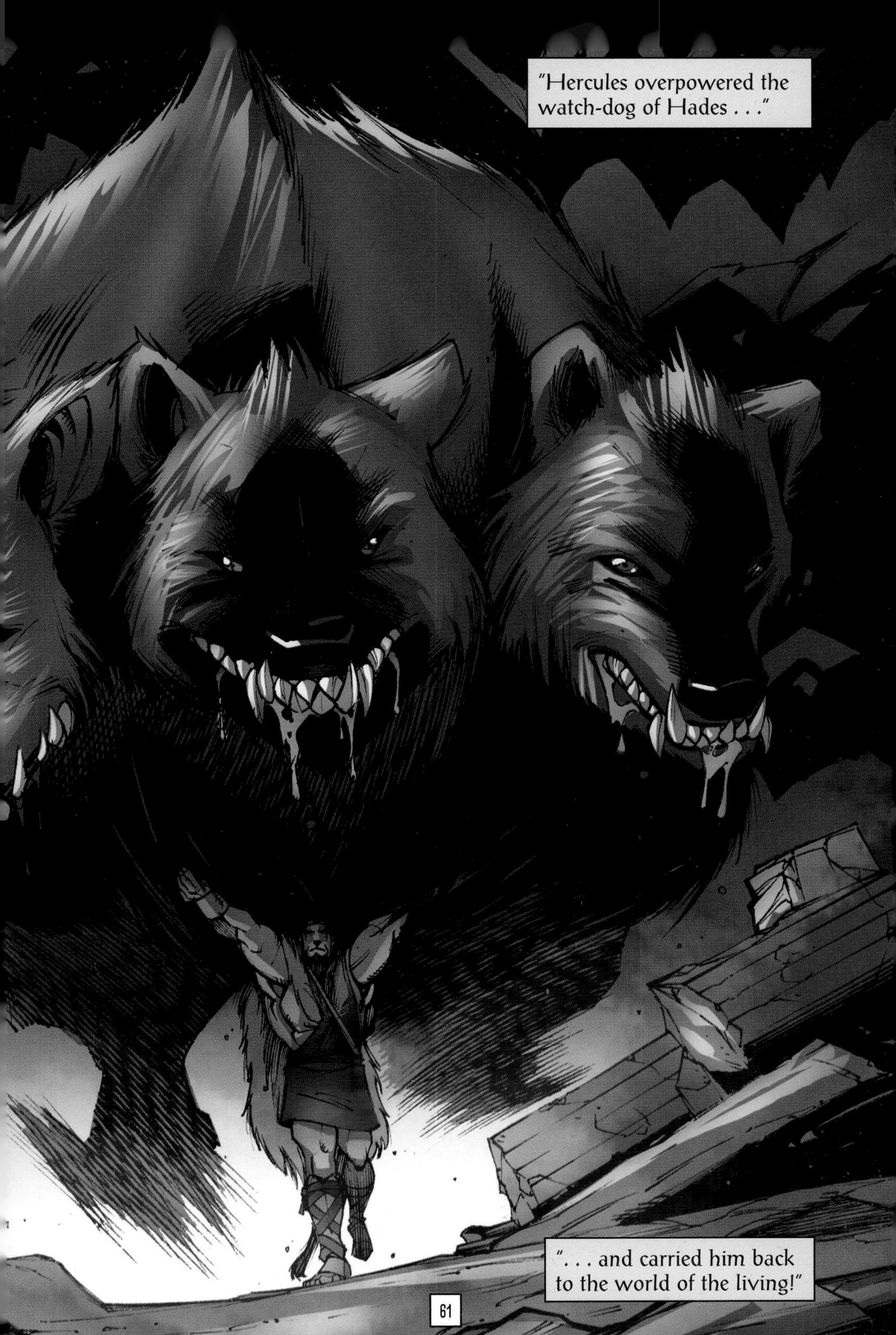
"Hercules overpowered the watch-dog of Hades . . ."
". . . and carried him back to the world of the living!"

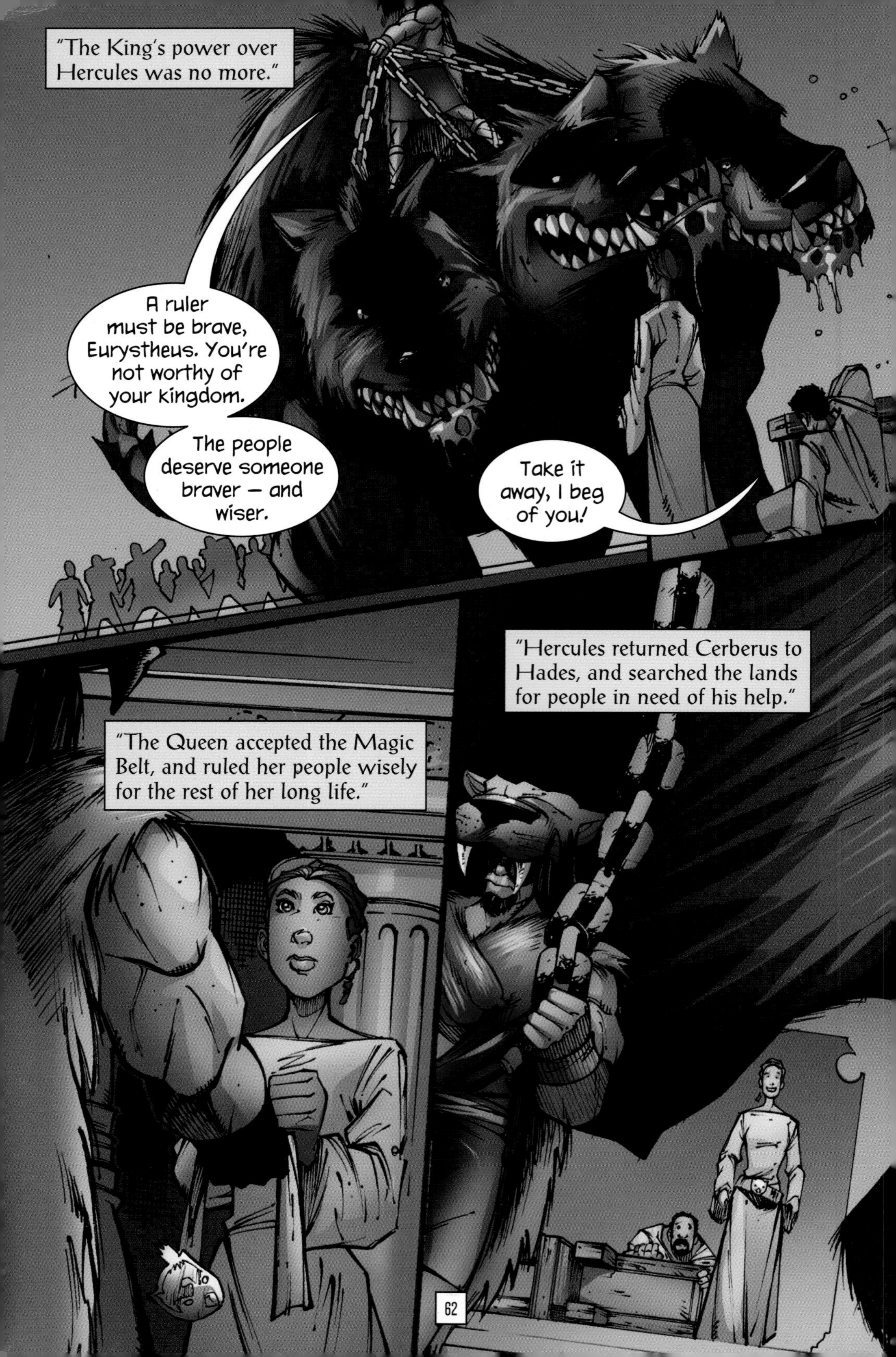
"The King's power over Hercules was no more."
A ruler must be brave, Eurystheus. You're not worthy of your kingdom.
The people deserve someone braver — and wiser.
Take it away, I beg of you!
"The Queen accepted the Magic Belt, and ruled her people wisely for the rest of her long life."
"Hercules returned Cerberus to Hades, and searched the lands for people in need of his help."

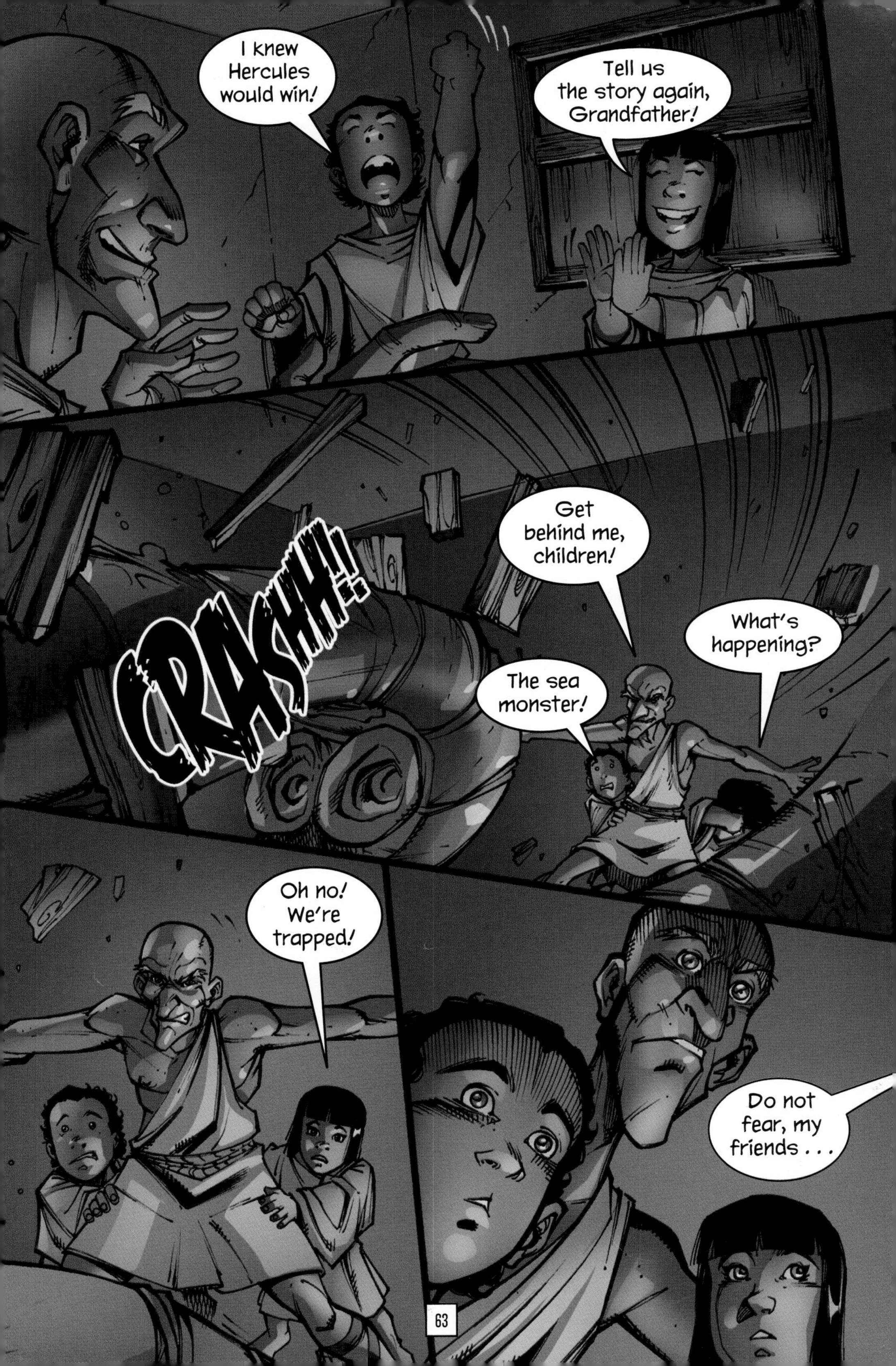
I knew Hercules would win!
Tell us the story again, Grandfather!
CRASHH!!
Get behind me, children!
What's happening?
The sea monster!
Oh no! We're trapped!
Do not fear, my friends . . .

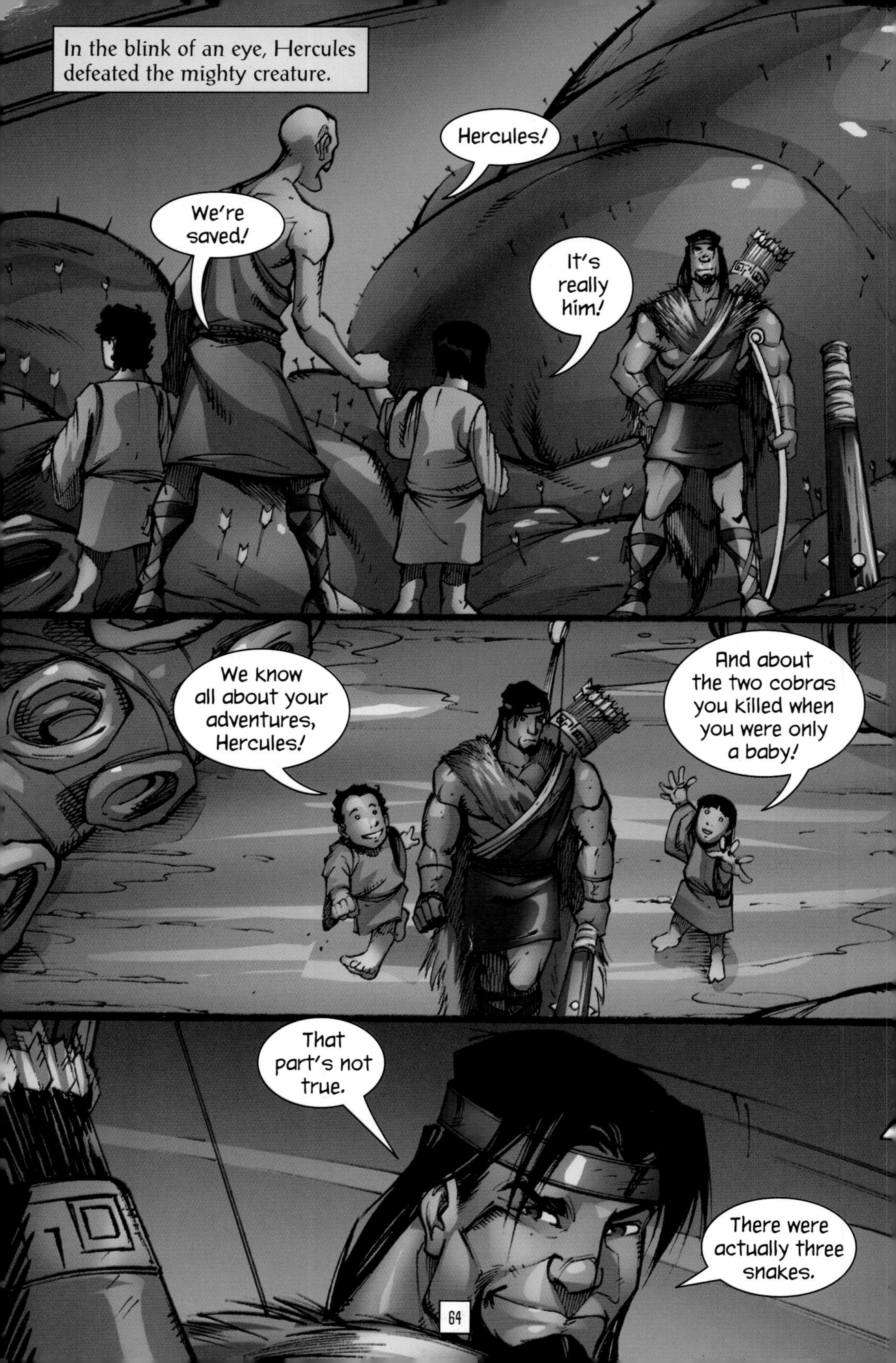
In the blink of an eye, Hercules defeated the mighty creature.
Hercules!
We're saved!
It's really him!
We know all about your adventures, Hercules!
And about the two cobras you killed when you were only a baby!
That part's not true.
There were actually three snakes.

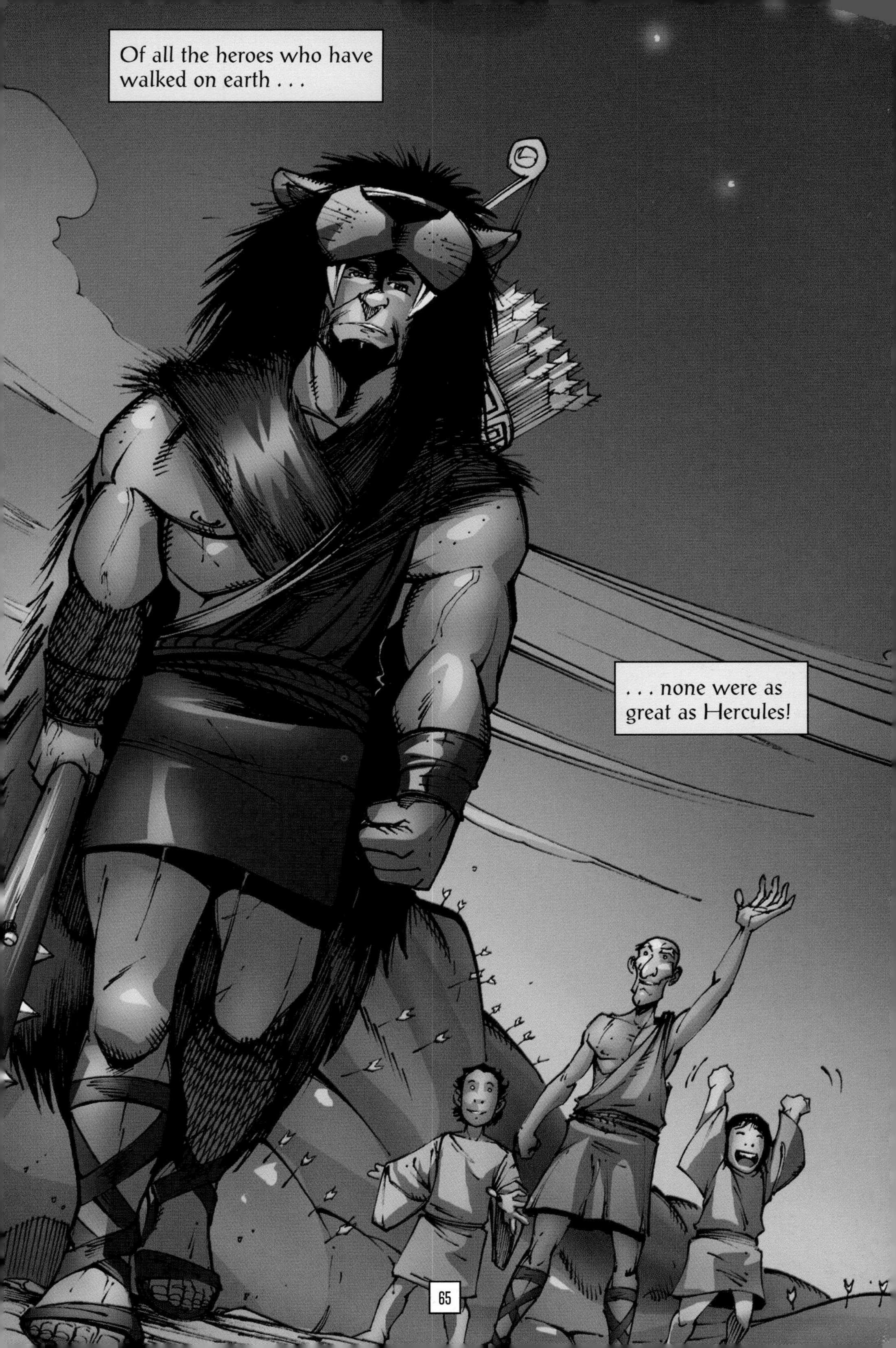
Of all the heroes who have walked on earth . . .
. . . none were as great as Hercules!

## ABOUT THE RETELLING AUTHOR

Since 1986, **Martin Powell** has been a freelance writer. He has written hundreds of stories, many of which have been published by Disney, Marvel, Tekno comic, Moonstone Books, and Capstone. In 1989, Powell received an Eisner Award nomination for his graphic novel *Scarlet in Gaslight*. This award is one of the highest comic book honors.

**José Alfonso Ocampo Ruiz** was born in 1975 in Macuspana, Tabasco in Mexico, where the temperature is just as hot as the sauce is. He became a comic book illustrator when he was 17 years old, and has worked on many graphic novels since then. Alfonso has illustrated several graphic novels, including retellings of *Dracula* and *Pinocchio*.

# GLOSSARY

**burden** (BUR-duhn)—a heavy load that someone has to carry, or something that someone is responsible for

**cruel** (KROO-uhl)—mean or unfair

**determination** (di-tur-min-NAY-shuhn)—having the will and desire to do something

**enchanted** (en-CHAN-tid)—a place or thing that has been put under a magic spell or seems magical

**eternity** (ee-TUR-nu-tee)—forever

**hexed** (HEKSD)—affected by an evil spell

**humiliate** (hyoo-MIL-ee-ate)—make someone feel foolish or embarrassed

**invulnerable** (in-VUHL-nur-uh-buhl)—unable to be hurt or harmed

**reputation** (rep-yuh-TAY-shuhn)—the way something or someone is seen by people

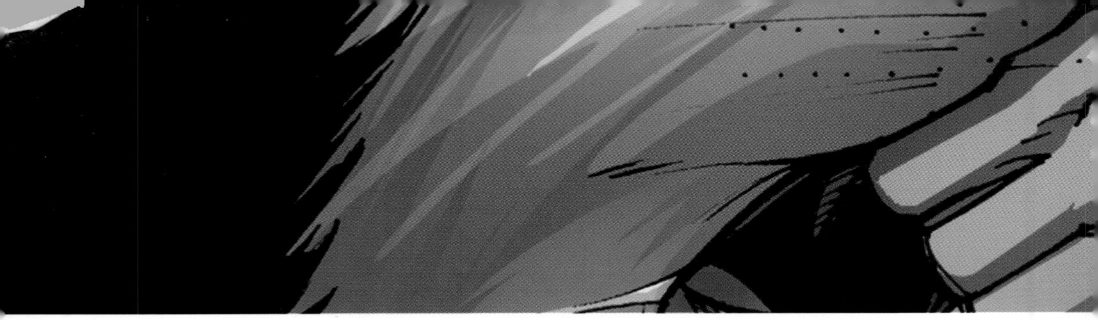

COMMON CORE ALIGNED
# READING QUESTIONS

1. **Are Hercules and King Eurystheus allies or rivals? Is Hercules a good guy or a bad guy? Is the King a bad guy or a good guy? How do you know?** *("Compare and contrast the point of view from which different stories are narrated.")*

2. ***The Adventures of Hercules* in graphic novel format is told as a "frame story." A frame story is a story within a story, offering the reader two levels of storytelling. What are the two stories in this graphic novel?** *("Refer to details and examples in a text when explaining what the text says explicitly and when drawing inferences from the text.")*

3. **Hercules is a true warrior. What does he do in the graphic novel to combat evil? Make sure to indicate specific pieces of art and text that support your answer.** *("Describe in depth a character . . . drawing on specific details in the text.")*

4. **Strength of mind and strength of body are two different themes in this book. What makes these two themes important? Find some important events and some important characters that demonstrate the importance of both mental and physical strength.** *("Determine a theme of a story.")*

5. **How do the images of Hercules portray his strength in battle? How does the text demonstrate Hercules strength? Compare and contrast the two.** *("Explain major differences between . . . structural elements.")*

# COMMON CORE ALIGNED
# WRITING QUESTIONS

1. If Hercules's father, Zeus, were a main character in the graphic novel, how might the story be told differently? What would Zeus say about all of Hercules's adventures and battles? (*"Orient the reader by establishing a situation and introducing a narrator."*)

2. Who do you think is more trustworthy? Hercules? The King? The Queen? Browse through the graphic novel a second time and find evidence to support your opinion. (*"Write opinion pieces on topics or texts, supporting a point of view with reasons and information."*)

3. Why is the King jealous of Hercules? Make a list of what Hercules does in this book that you think makes the King jealous. (*"Draw evidence from literary . . . texts to support analysis."*)

4. Is there a bully in this book? How do you know? Write down some page numbers or quotations from the text to support your answer. (*"Describe in depth a character . . . drawing on specific details in the text."*)

5. The King has asked you to write a "Wanted!" poster for Hercules. Be sure to use images and words that will get right to the point about why Hercules is wanted. Feel free to use various images of Hercules from the graphic novel to inspire your poster picture. (*"Produce clear and coherent writing in which the development and organization are appropriate to task, purpose, and audience."*)

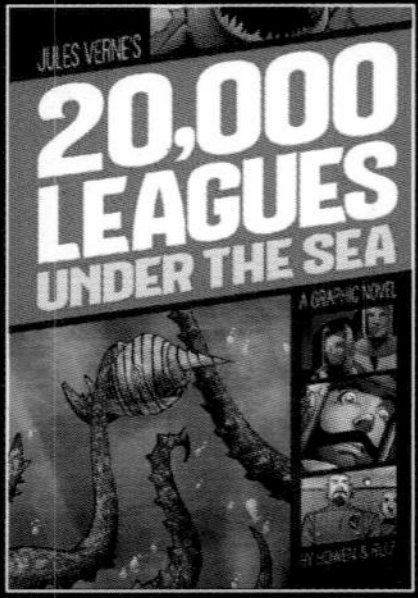
JULES VERNE'S
20,000 LEAGUES UNDER THE SEA
A GRAPHIC NOVEL

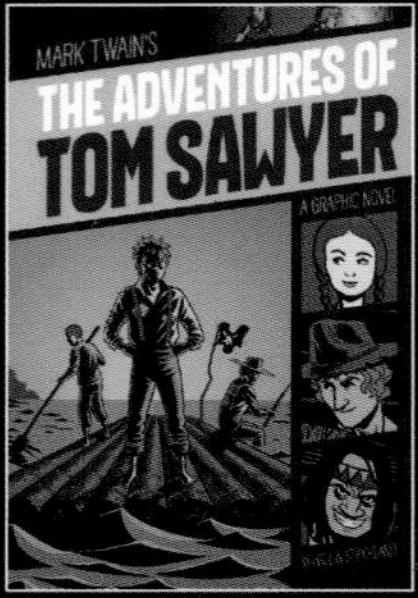
MARK TWAIN'S
THE ADVENTURES OF TOM SAWYER
A GRAPHIC NOVEL

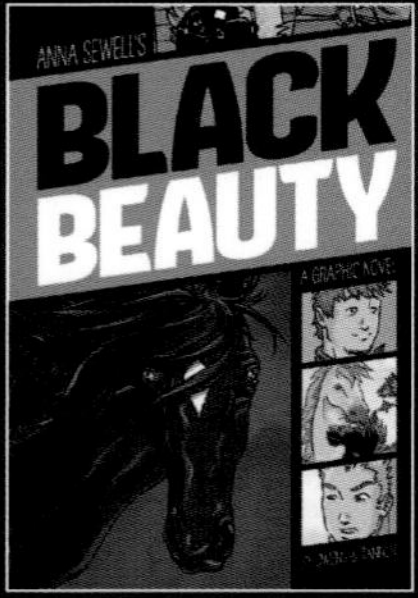
ANNA SEWELL'S
BLACK BEAUTY
A GRAPHIC NOVEL

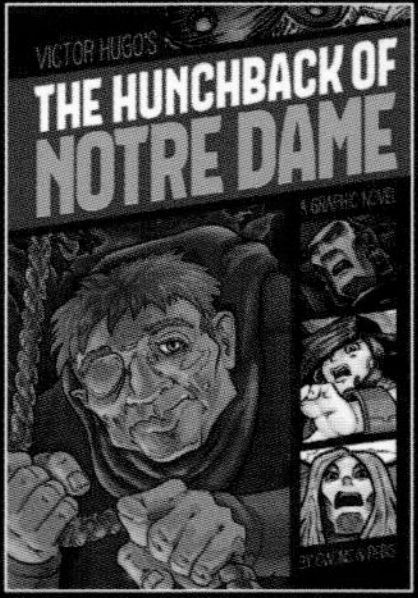
VICTOR HUGO'S
THE HUNCHBACK OF NOTRE DAME
A GRAPHIC NOVEL

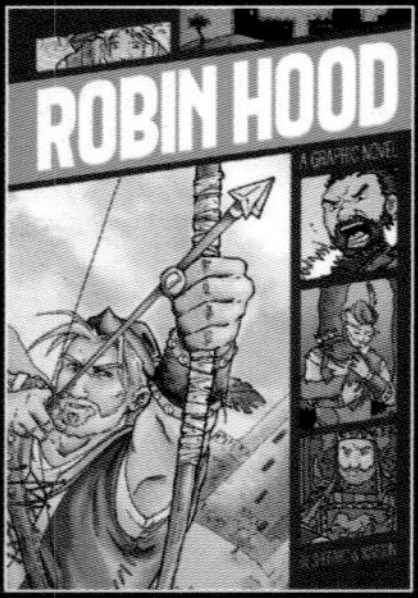
ROBIN HOOD
A GRAPHIC NOVEL

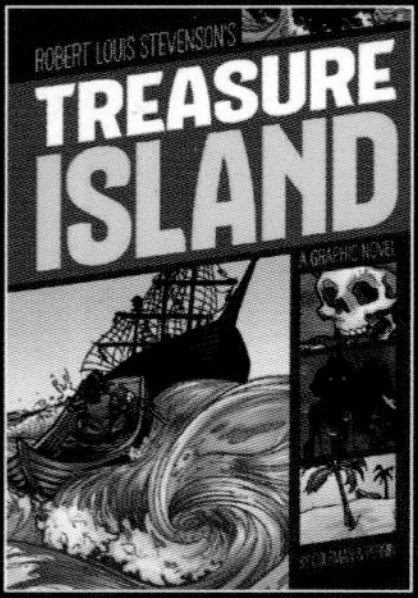
ROBERT LOUIS STEVENSON'S
TREASURE ISLAND
A GRAPHIC NOVEL

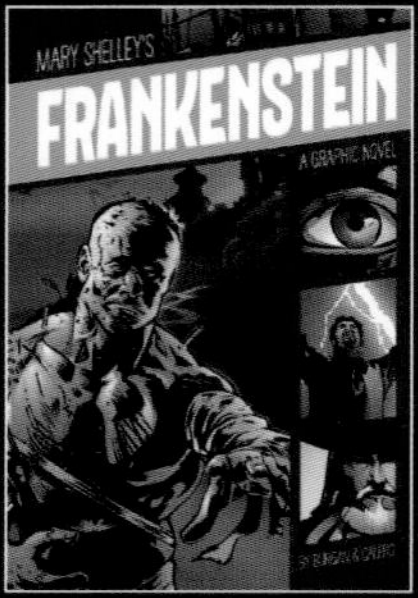
MARY SHELLEY'S
FRANKENSTEIN
A GRAPHIC NOVEL

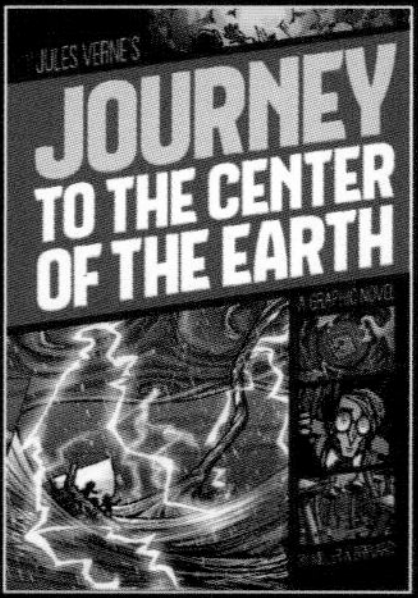
JULES VERNE'S
JOURNEY TO THE CENTER OF THE EARTH
A GRAPHIC NOVEL

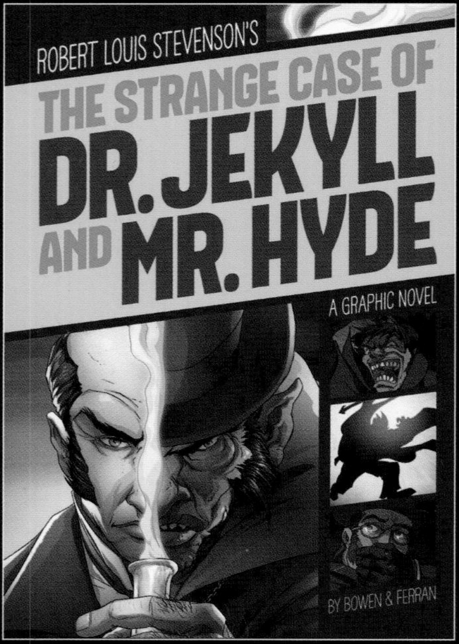
ROBERT LOUIS STEVENSON'S
THE STRANGE CASE OF DR. JEKYLL AND MR. HYDE
A GRAPHIC NOVEL
BY BOWEN & FERRAN

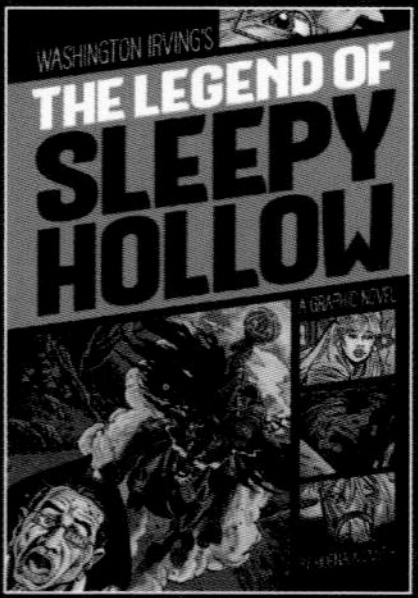
WASHINGTON IRVING'S
THE LEGEND OF SLEEPY HOLLOW
A GRAPHIC NOVEL

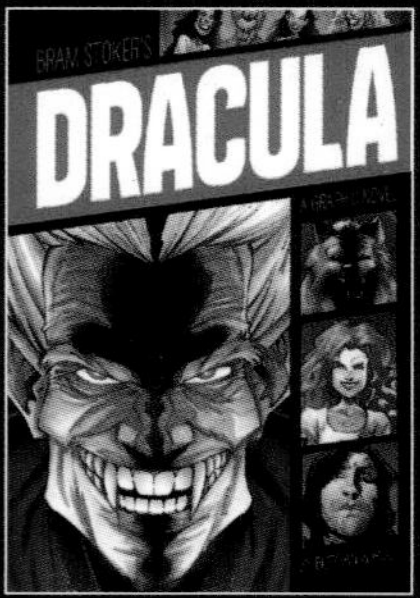
BRAM STOKER'S
DRACULA

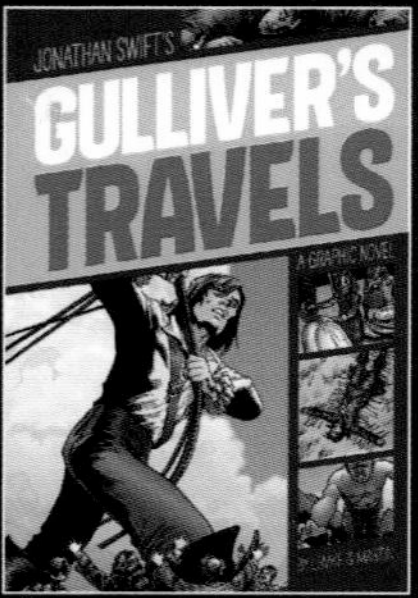
JONATHAN SWIFT'S
GULLIVER'S TRAVELS
A GRAPHIC NOVEL

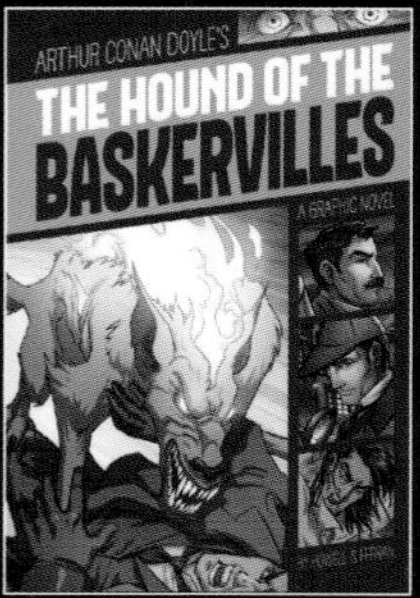
ARTHUR CONAN DOYLE'S
THE HOUND OF THE BASKERVILLES
A GRAPHIC NOVEL

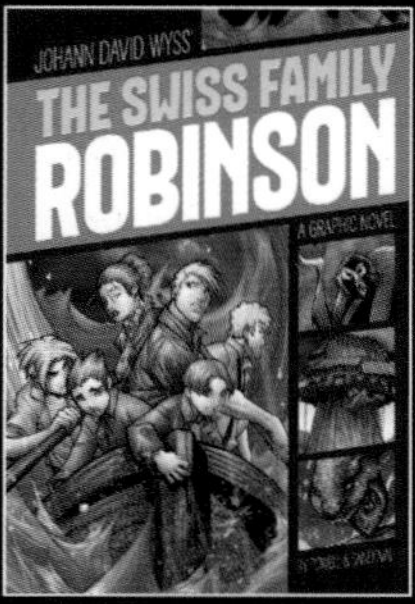
JOHANN DAVID WYSS
THE SWISS FAMILY ROBINSON
A GRAPHIC NOVEL
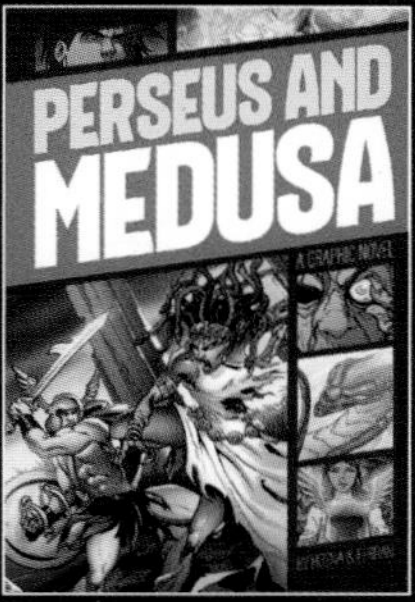
PERSEUS AND MEDUSA
A GRAPHIC NOVEL
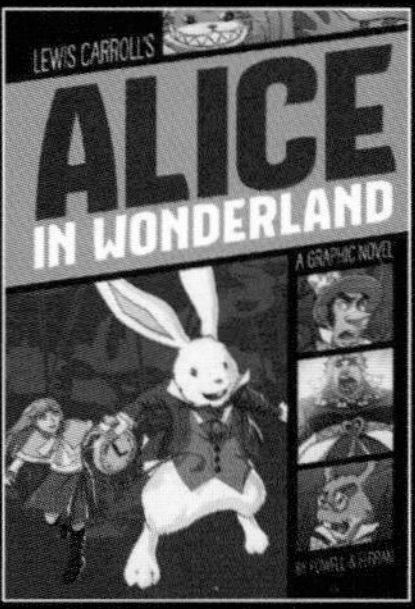
LEWIS CARROLL'S
ALICE IN WONDERLAND
A GRAPHIC NOVEL
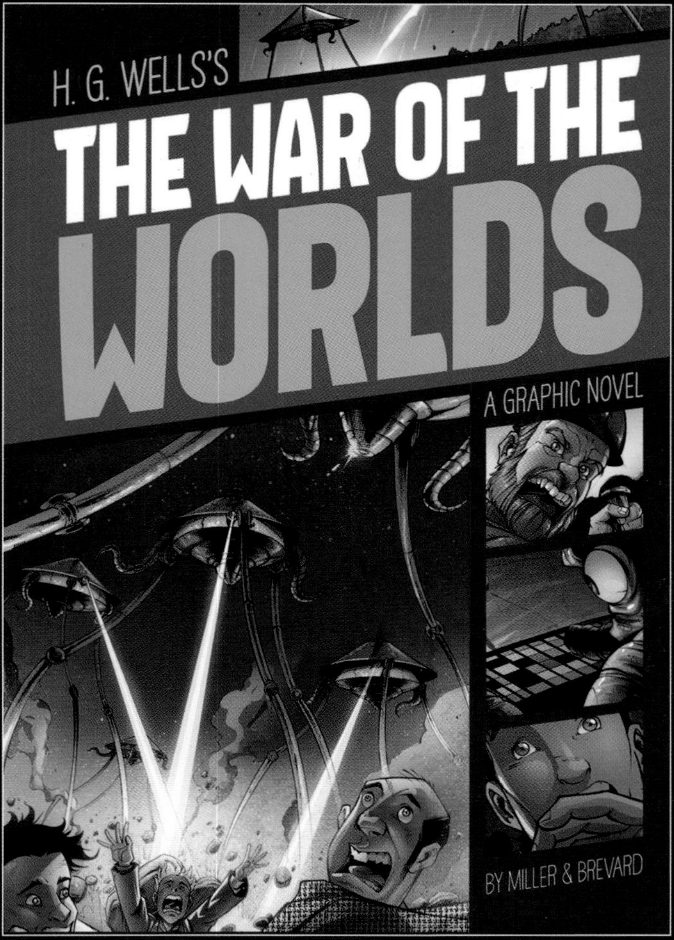
H. G. WELLS'S
THE WAR OF THE WORLDS
A GRAPHIC NOVEL
BY MILLER & BREVARD
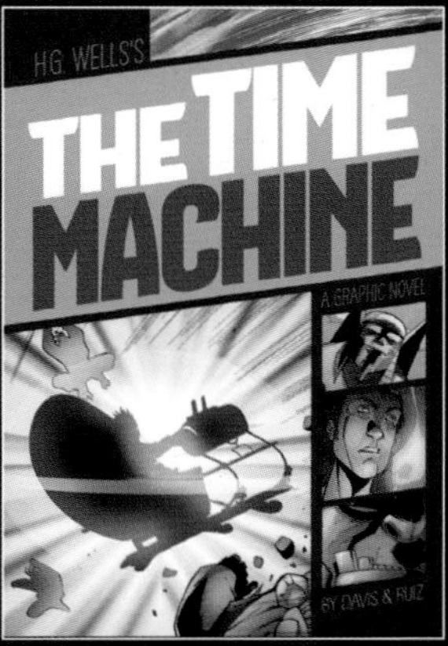
H.G. WELLS'S
THE TIME MACHINE
A GRAPHIC NOVEL
BY DAVIS & RUIZ
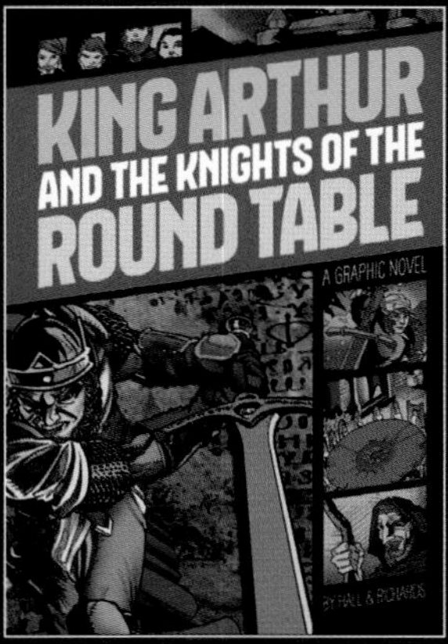
KING ARTHUR AND THE KNIGHTS OF THE ROUND TABLE
A GRAPHIC NOVEL
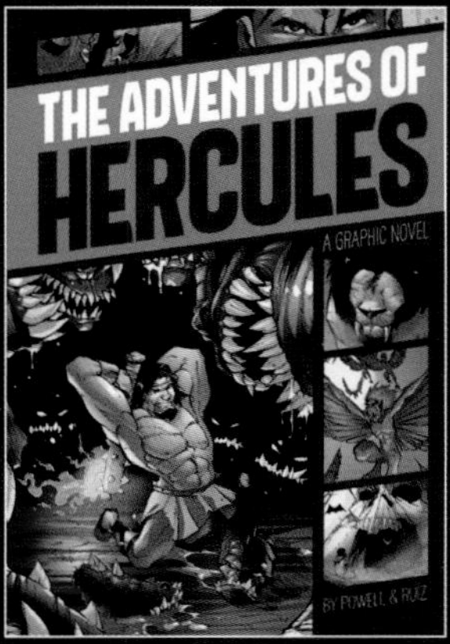
THE ADVENTURES OF HERCULES
A GRAPHIC NOVEL
BY POWELL & RUIZ